POKÉMON™

BLACK AND WHITE

VOL.20

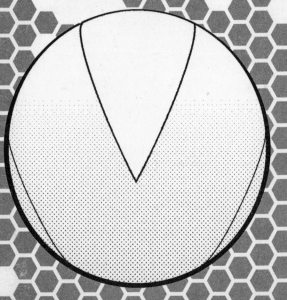

Story by **HIDENORI KUSAKA**
Art by **SATOSHI YAMAMOTO**

Pokémon Black and White
Volume 20
Perfect Square Edition

Story by HIDENORI KUSAKA
Art by SATOSHI YAMAMOTO

© 2015 Pokémon.
© 1995–2015 Nintendo/Creatures Inc./GAME FREAK inc.
TM, ®, and character names are trademarks of Nintendo.
POCKET MONSTERS SPECIAL (Magazine Edition)
by Hidenori KUSAKA, Satoshi YAMAMOTO
© 1997 Hidenori KUSAKA, Satoshi YAMAMOTO
All rights reserved.
Original Japanese edition published by SHOGAKUKAN.
English translation rights in the United States of America, Canada, the United Kingdom,
Ireland, Australia and New Zealand arranged with SHOGAKUKAN.

English Adaptation / Bryant Turnage
Translation / Tetsuichiro Miyaki
Touch-up & Lettering / Susan Daigle-Leach
Design / Fawn Lau
Editor / Annette Roman

Printed in the U.S.A.

Published by VIZ Media, LLC
P.O. Box 77010
San Francisco, CA 94107

10 9 8 7 6 5 4 3 2 1
First printing, February 2015

www.perfectsquare.com

www.viz.com

POKÉMON™ BLACK AND WHITE

VOL. 20

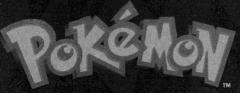

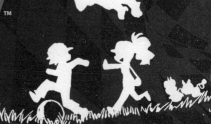

THE STORY THUS FAR!

Pokémon Trainer Black is exploring the mysterious Unova region with his brand-new Pokédex. Pokémon Trainer White runs a thriving talent agency for performing Pokémon. While traveling together, their paths cross with Team Plasma, a nefarious group that advocates releasing your Pokémon into the wild! Now Black and White are off on their own separate journeys of discovery...

BLACK'S dream is to win the Pokémon League!

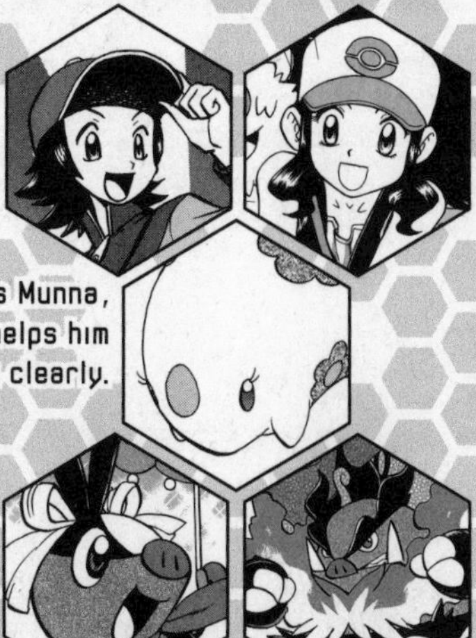

WHITE'S dream is to work in show biz... and now she's learning how to Pokémon Battle as well!

Black's Munna, MUSHA, helps him think clearly.

White's Tepig, GIGI, and Black's Emboar, BO, get along like peanut butter and jelly!

Adventure 64 The Battle

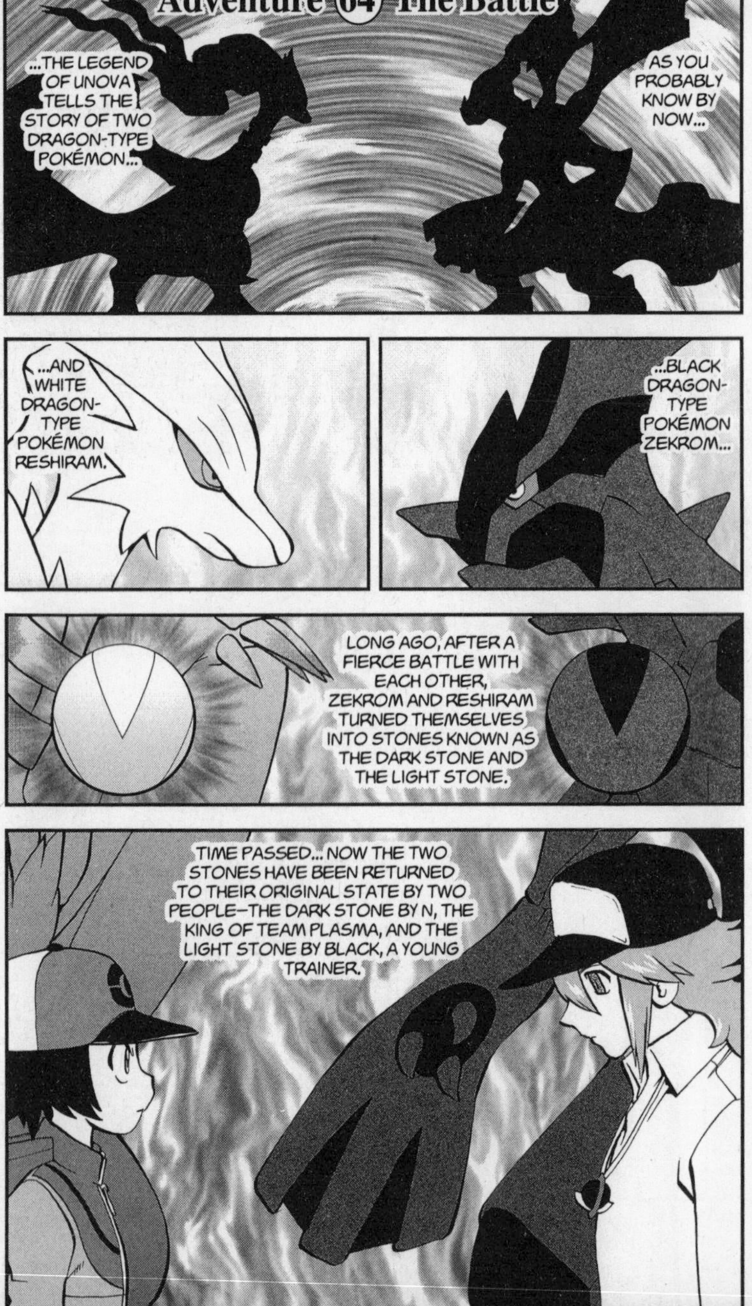
AS YOU PROBABLY KNOW BY NOW...
...THE LEGEND OF UNOVA TELLS THE STORY OF TWO DRAGON-TYPE POKÉMON...
...BLACK DRAGON-TYPE POKÉMON ZEKROM...
...AND WHITE DRAGON-TYPE POKÉMON RESHIRAM.
LONG AGO, AFTER A FIERCE BATTLE WITH EACH OTHER, ZEKROM AND RESHIRAM TURNED THEMSELVES INTO STONES KNOWN AS THE DARK STONE AND THE LIGHT STONE.
TIME PASSED... NOW THE TWO STONES HAVE BEEN RETURNED TO THEIR ORIGINAL STATE BY TWO PEOPLE—THE DARK STONE BY N, THE KING OF TEAM PLASMA, AND THE LIGHT STONE BY BLACK, A YOUNG TRAINER.

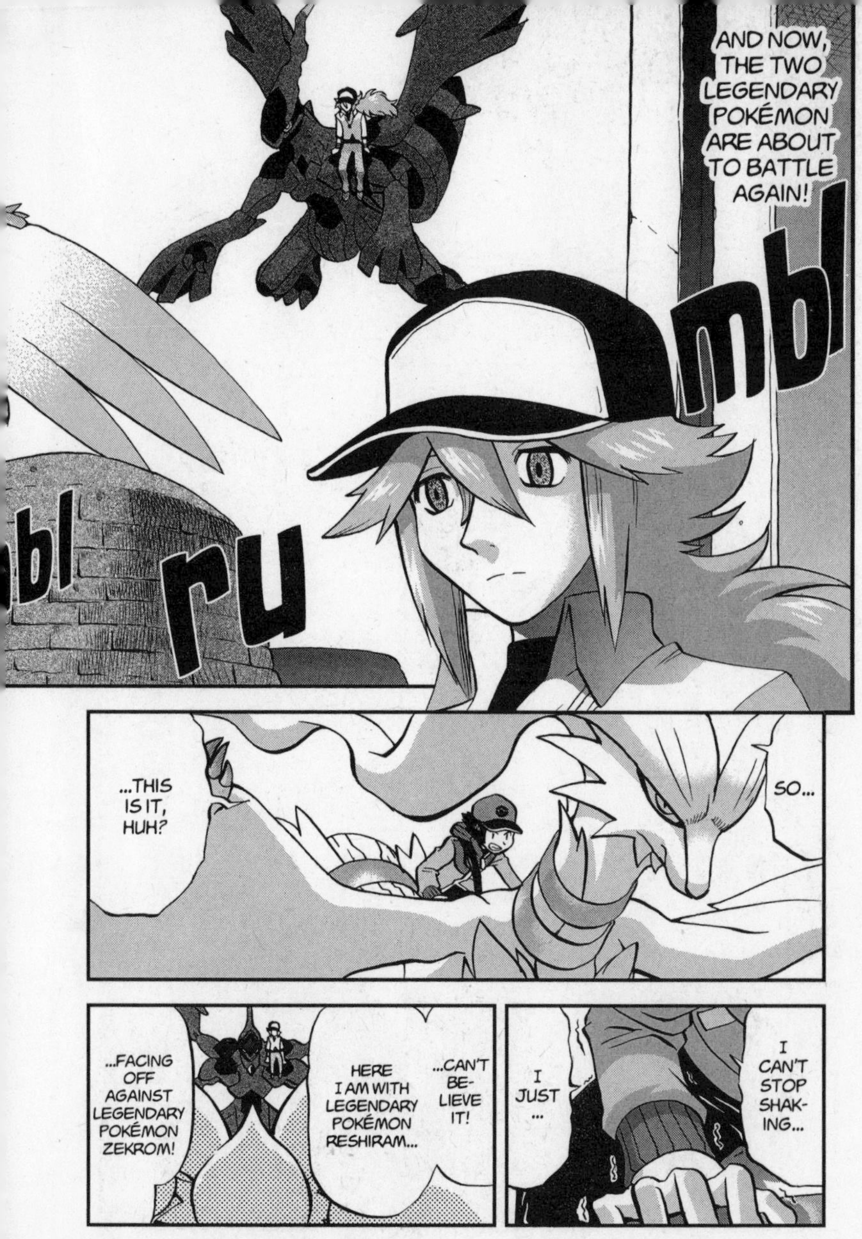
AND NOW, THE TWO LEGENDARY POKÉMON ARE ABOUT TO BATTLE AGAIN!
mbl
ru
bl
SO...
...THIS IS IT, HUH?
I CAN'T STOP SHAKING...
I JUST ...
...CAN'T BELIEVE IT!
HERE I AM WITH LEGENDARY POKÉMON RESHIRAM...
...FACING OFF AGAINST LEGENDARY POKÉMON ZEKROM!

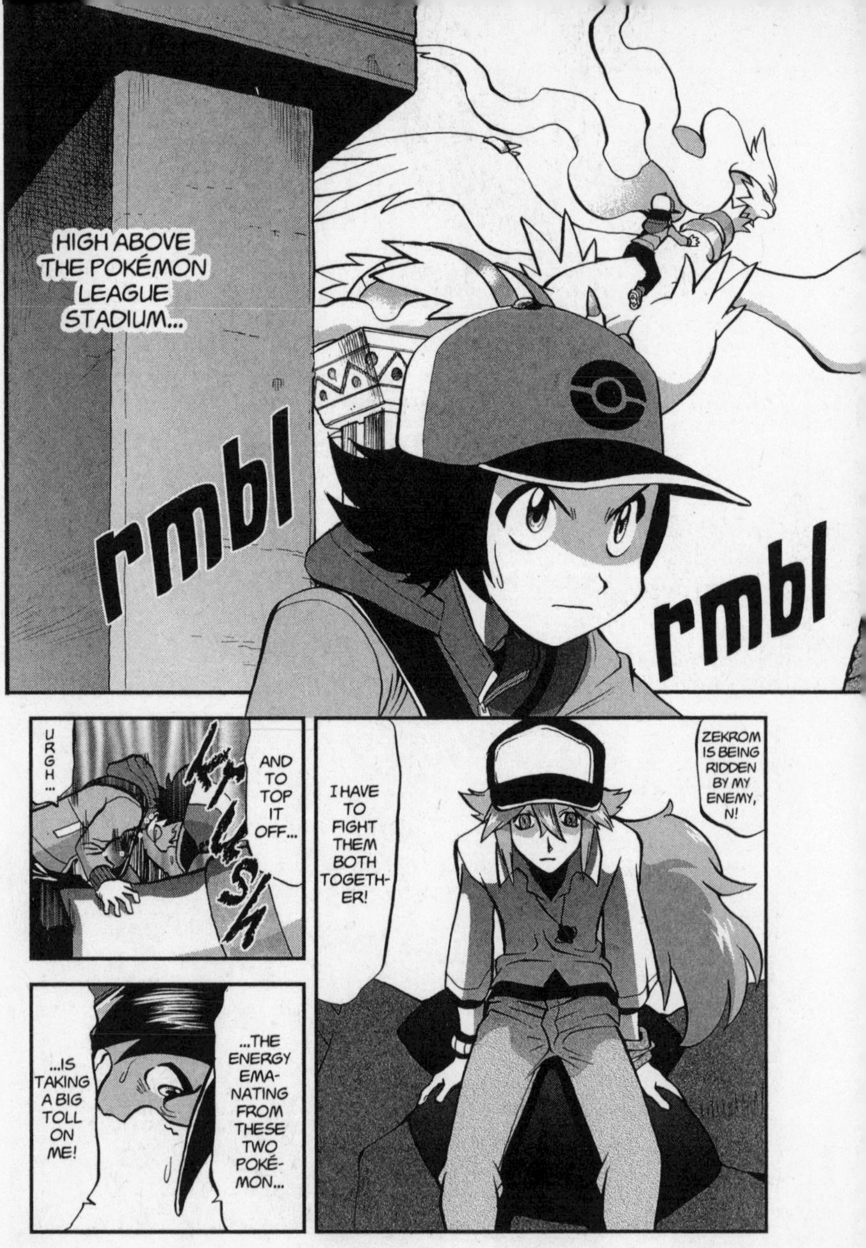
HIGH ABOVE THE POKÉMON LEAGUE STADIUM...
rmbl
rmbl
ZEKROM IS BEING RIDDEN BY MY ENEMY, N!
I HAVE TO FIGHT THEM BOTH TOGETH-ER!
AND TO TOP IT OFF...
URGH...
...THE ENERGY EMA-NATING FROM THESE TWO POKÉ-MON...
...IS TAKING A BIG TOLL ON ME!

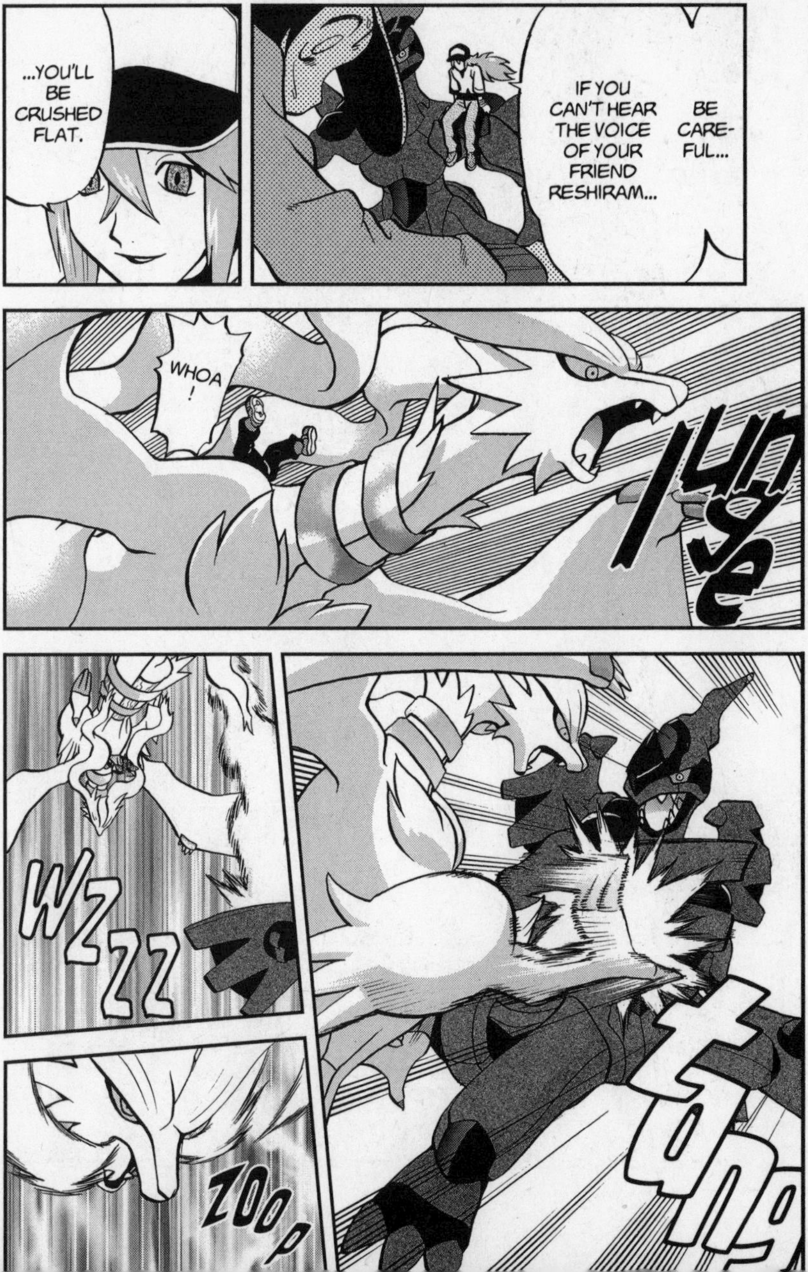
BE CARE-FUL...
IF YOU CAN'T HEAR THE VOICE OF YOUR FRIEND RESHIRAM...
...YOU'LL BE CRUSHED FLAT.
WHOA!
lunge
WZZZ
ZOOP

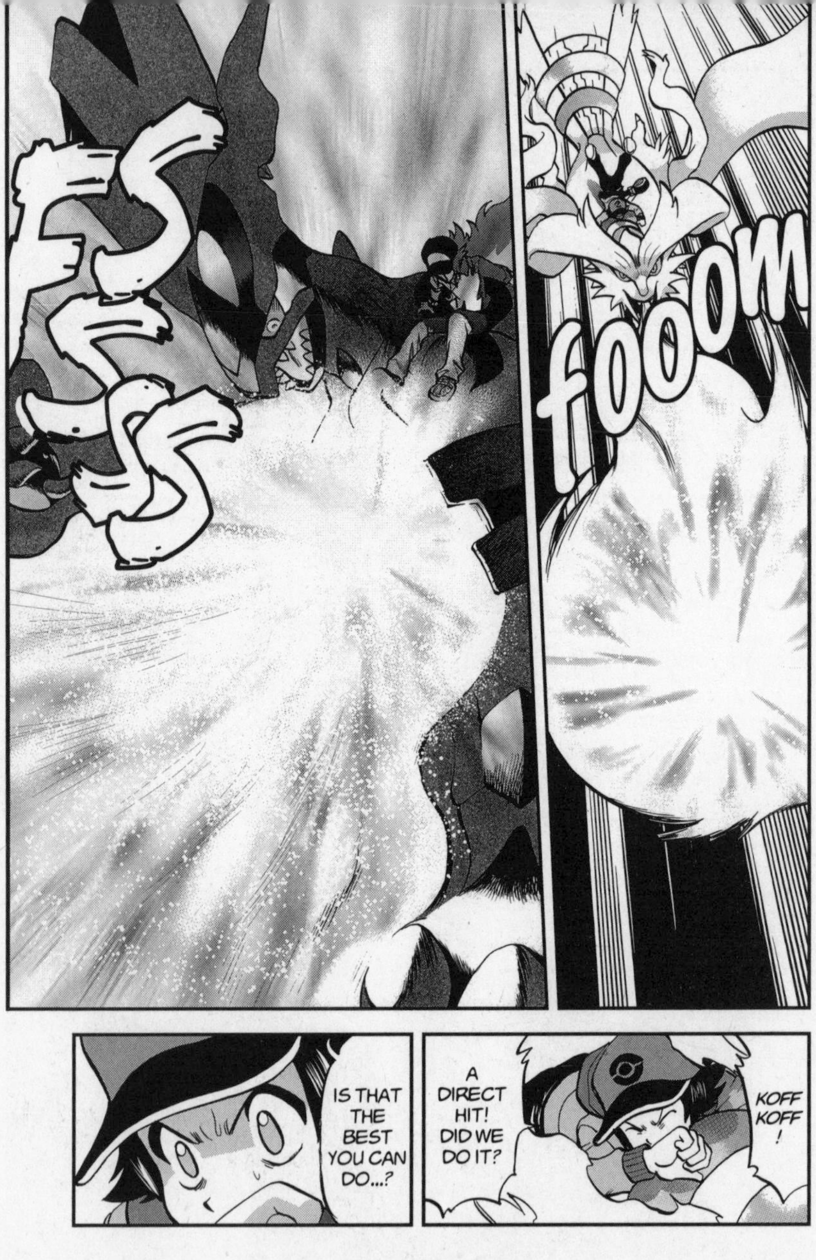
FOOOM
FSSS
KOFF KOFF!
A DIRECT HIT! DID WE DO IT?
IS THAT THE BEST YOU CAN DO...?

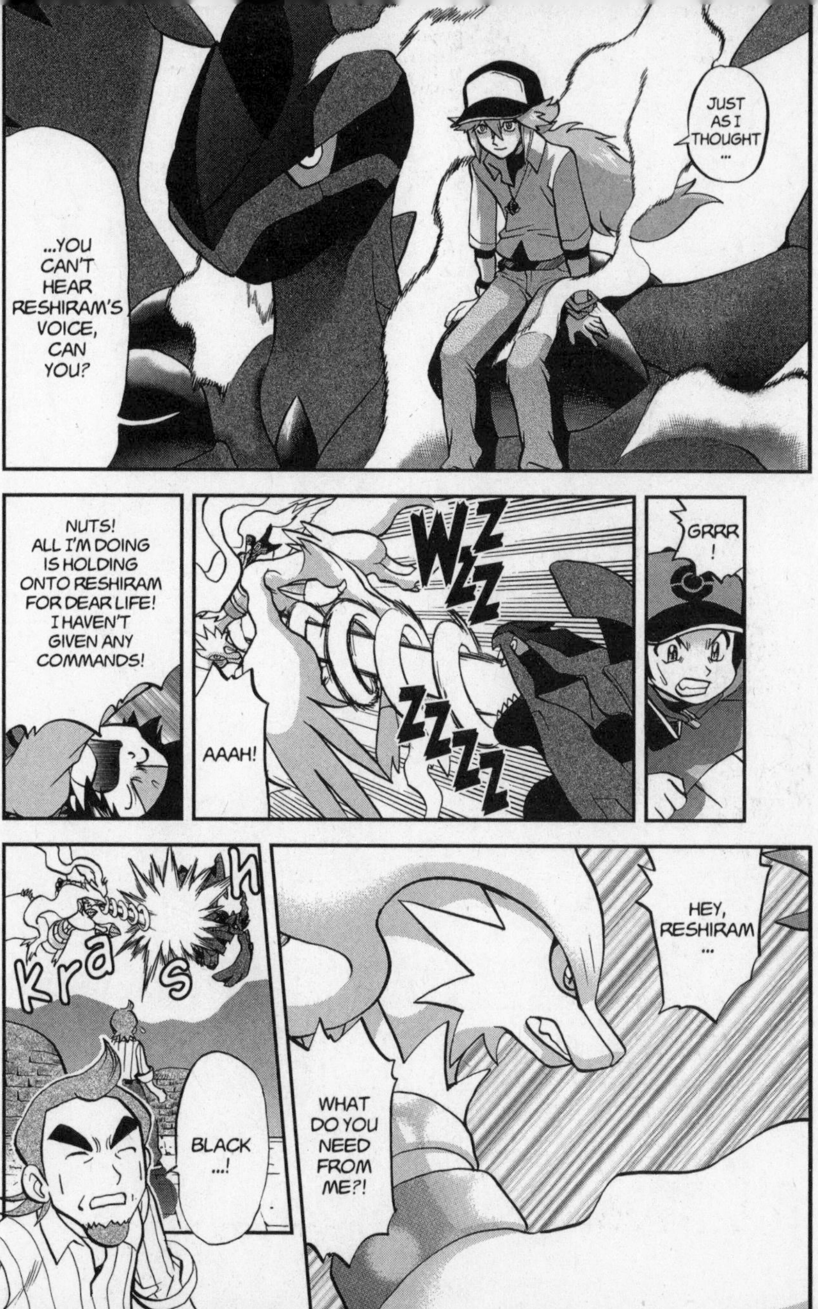
JUST AS I THOUGHT ...
...YOU CAN'T HEAR RESHIRAM'S VOICE, CAN YOU?
GRRR!
WZZZZZZZZ
AAAH!
NUTS! ALL I'M DOING IS HOLDING ONTO RESHIRAM FOR DEAR LIFE! I HAVEN'T GIVEN ANY COMMANDS!
HEY, RESHIRAM ...
WHAT DO YOU NEED FROM ME?!
Krash
BLACK ...!

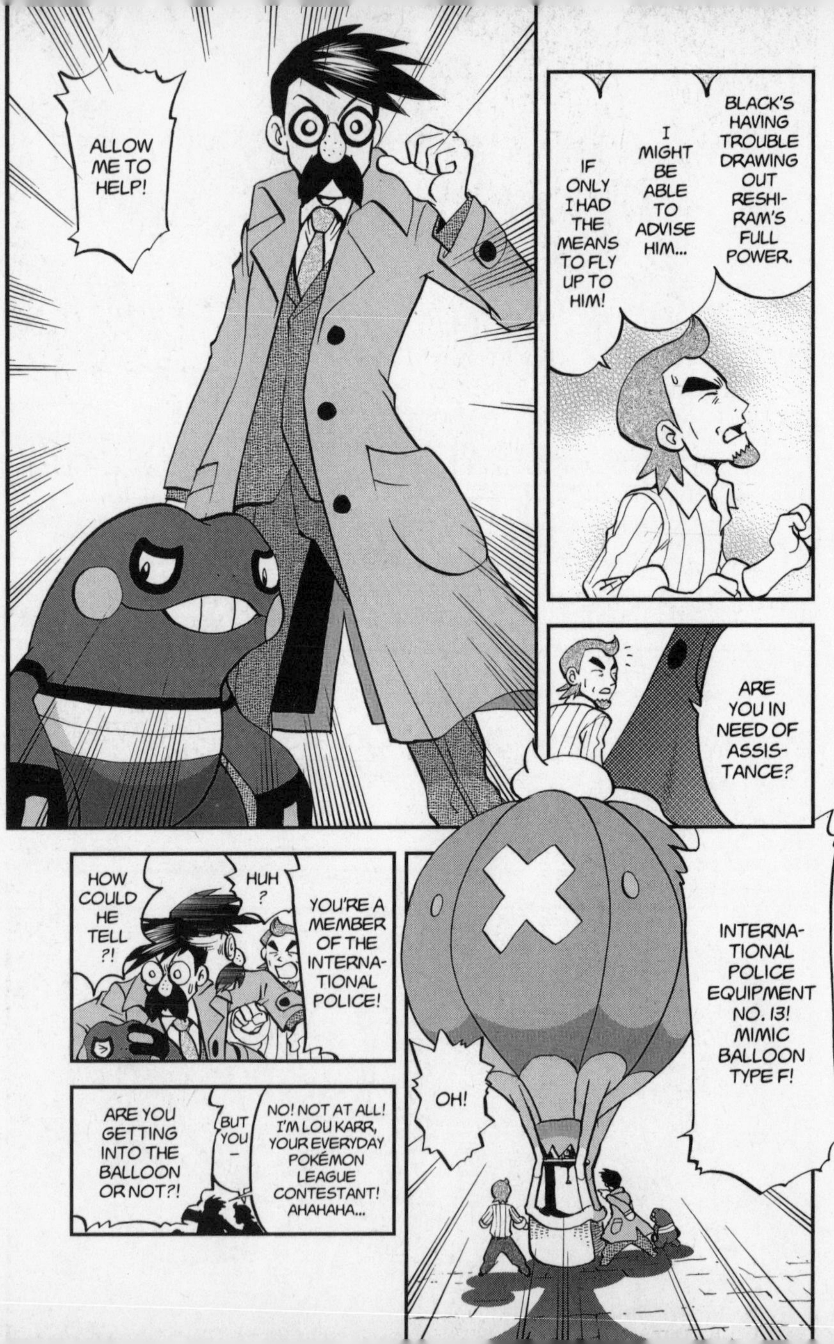
BLACK'S HAVING TROUBLE DRAWING OUT RESHI-RAM'S FULL POWER.
I MIGHT BE ABLE TO ADVISE HIM...
IF ONLY I HAD THE MEANS TO FLY UP TO HIM!
ARE YOU IN NEED OF ASSIS-TANCE?
ALLOW ME TO HELP!
INTERNA-TIONAL POLICE EQUIPMENT NO. 13! MIMIC BALLOON TYPE F!
OH!
YOU'RE A MEMBER OF THE INTERNA-TIONAL POLICE!
HUH?
HOW COULD HE TELL?!
NO! NOT AT ALL! I'M LOU KARR, YOUR EVERYDAY POKÉMON LEAGUE CONTESTANT! AHAHAHA...
BUT YOU—
ARE YOU GETTING INTO THE BALLOON OR NOT?!

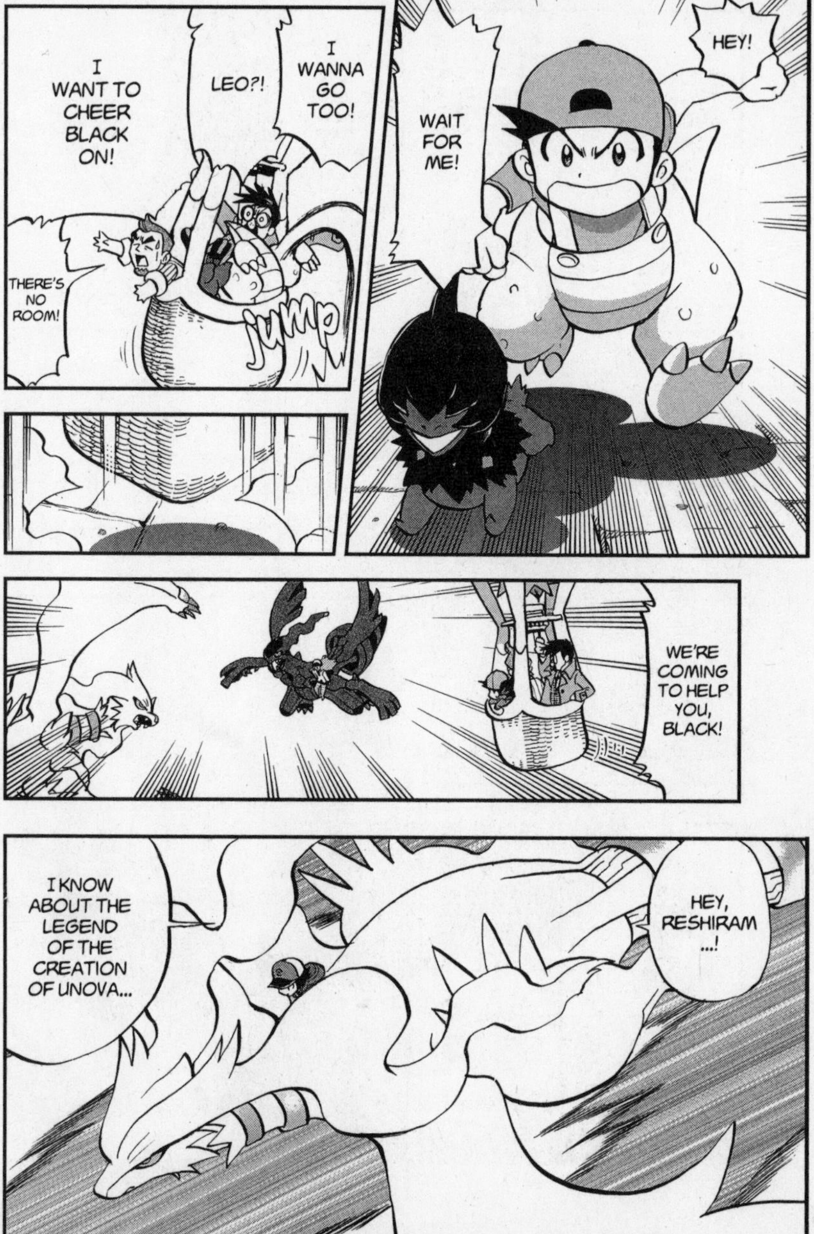
HEY!
WAIT FOR ME!
I WANNA GO TOO!
LEO?!
I WANT TO CHEER BLACK ON!
THERE'S NO ROOM!
jump
WE'RE COMING TO HELP YOU, BLACK!
HEY, RESHIRAM ...!
I KNOW ABOUT THE LEGEND OF THE CREATION OF UNOVA...

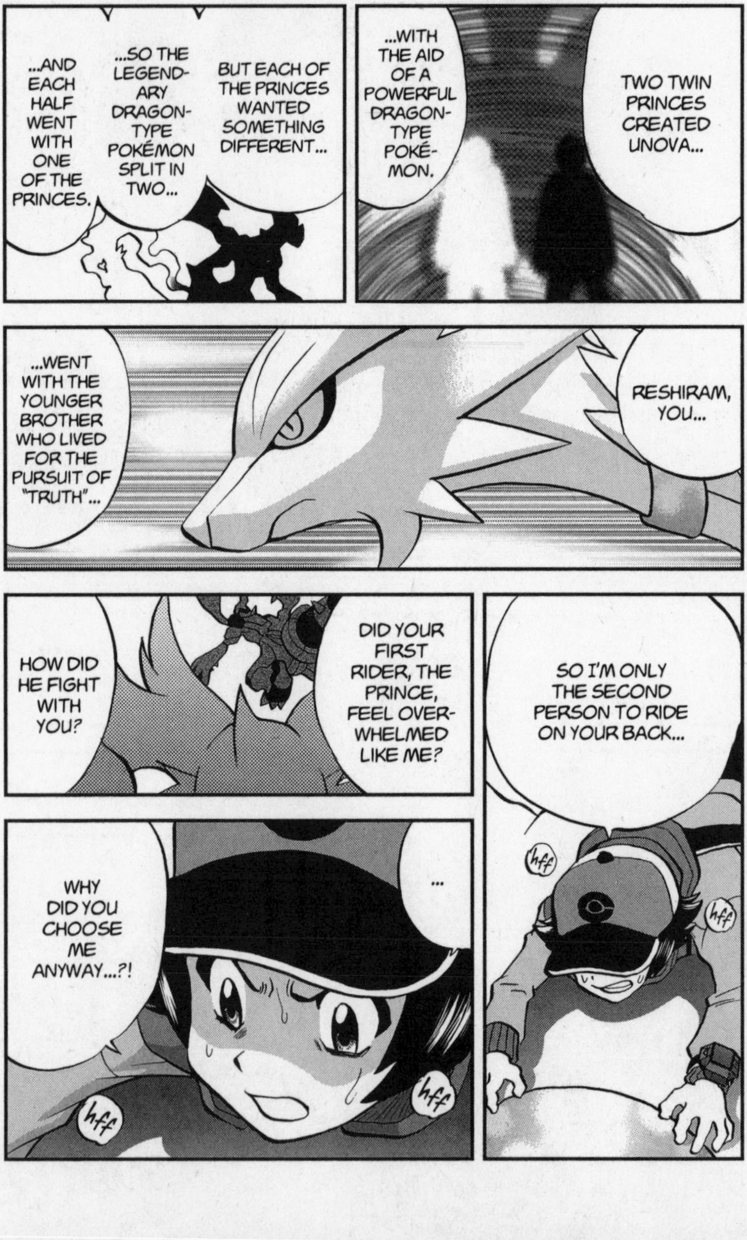
TWO TWIN PRINCES CREATED UNOVA...
...WITH THE AID OF A POWERFUL DRAGON-TYPE POKÉMON.
BUT EACH OF THE PRINCES WANTED SOMETHING DIFFERENT...
...SO THE LEGENDARY DRAGON-TYPE POKÉMON SPLIT IN TWO...
...AND EACH HALF WENT WITH ONE OF THE PRINCES.
RESHIRAM, YOU...
...WENT WITH THE YOUNGER BROTHER WHO LIVED FOR THE PURSUIT OF "TRUTH"...
SO I'M ONLY THE SECOND PERSON TO RIDE ON YOUR BACK...
hff
hff
DID YOUR FIRST RIDER, THE PRINCE, FEEL OVERWHELMED LIKE ME?
HOW DID HE FIGHT WITH YOU?
...
WHY DID YOU CHOOSE ME ANYWAY...?!
hff
hff

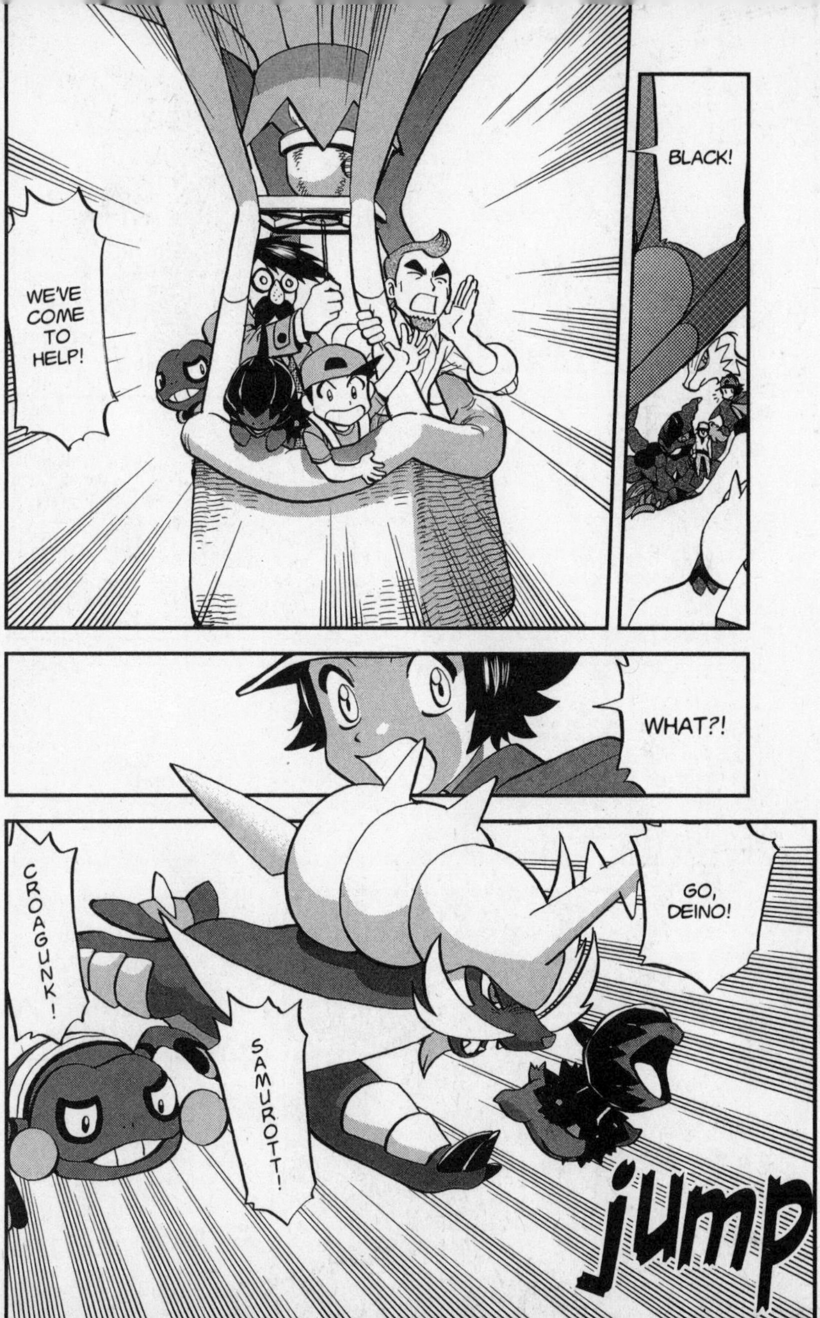
BLACK!
WE'VE COME TO HELP!
WHAT?!
GO, DEINO!
CROAGUNK!
SAMUROTT!
jump

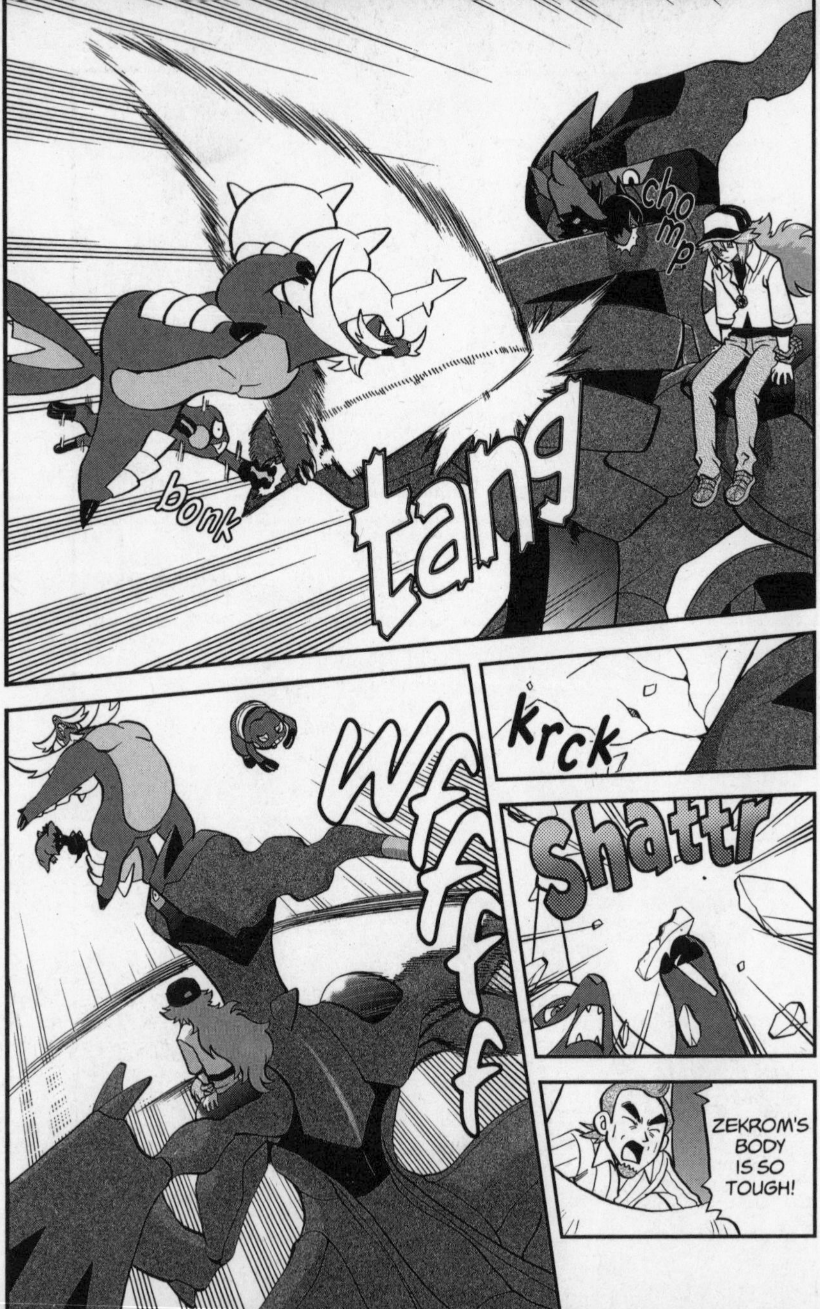
chomp
tang
bonk
krck
shattr
ZEKROM'S BODY IS SO TOUGH!
Wffff

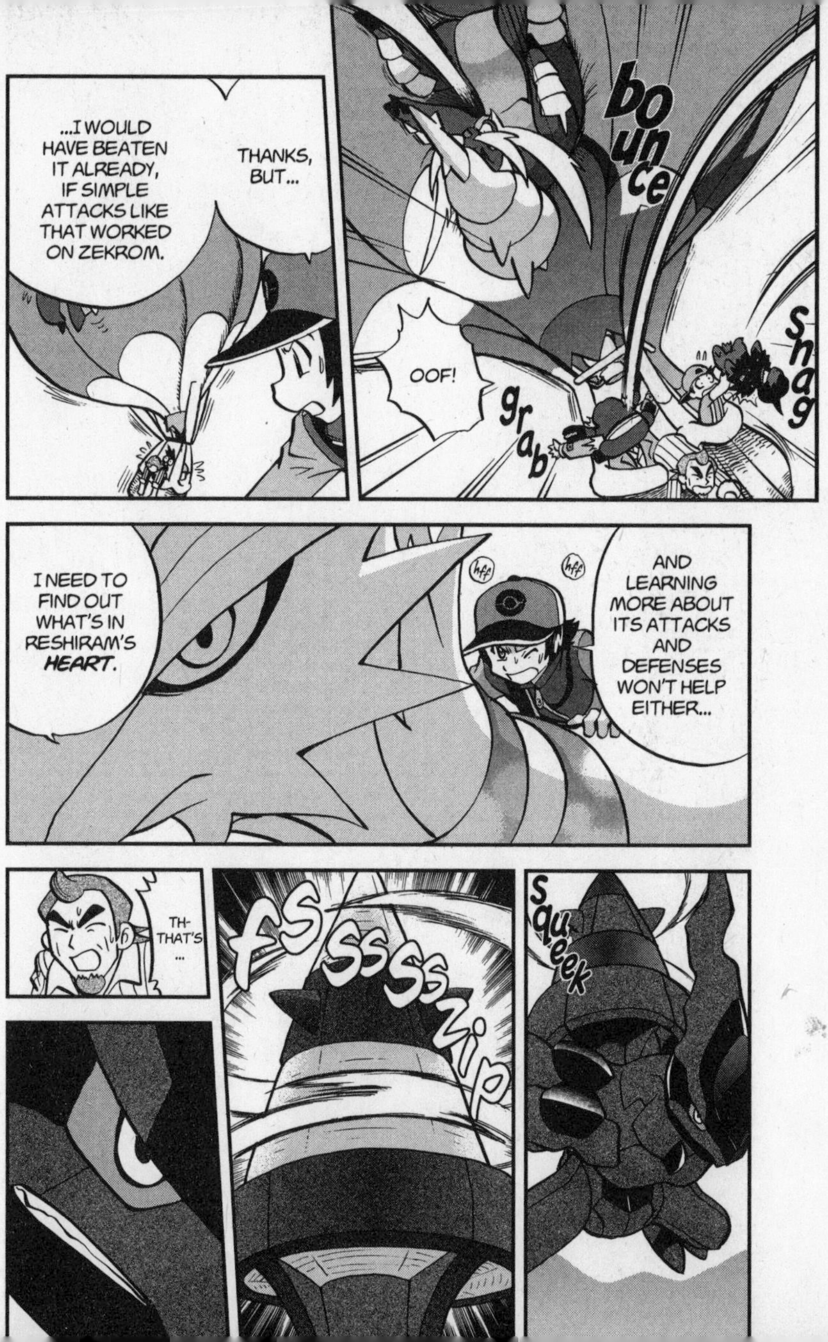
bounce
OOF!
grab
snag
THANKS, BUT...
...I WOULD HAVE BEATEN IT ALREADY, IF SIMPLE ATTACKS LIKE THAT WORKED ON ZEKROM.
hff
hff
AND LEARNING MORE ABOUT ITS ATTACKS AND DEFENSES WON'T HELP EITHER...
I NEED TO FIND OUT WHAT'S IN RESHIRAM'S ***HEART***.
squeeek
fsssssszip
TH-THAT'S ...

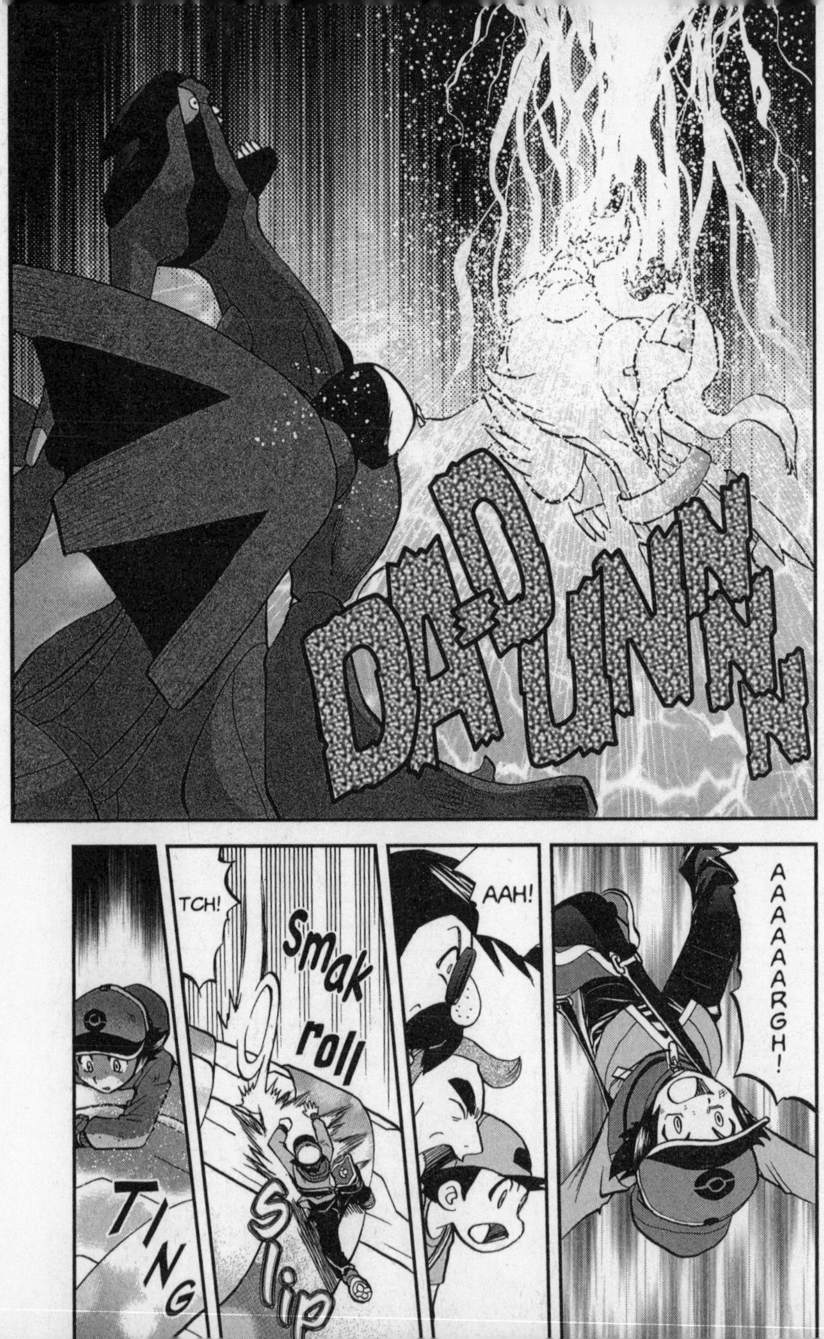
DADUNNN
AAAAAAARGH!
AAH!
TCH!
Smak
roll
Slip
TING

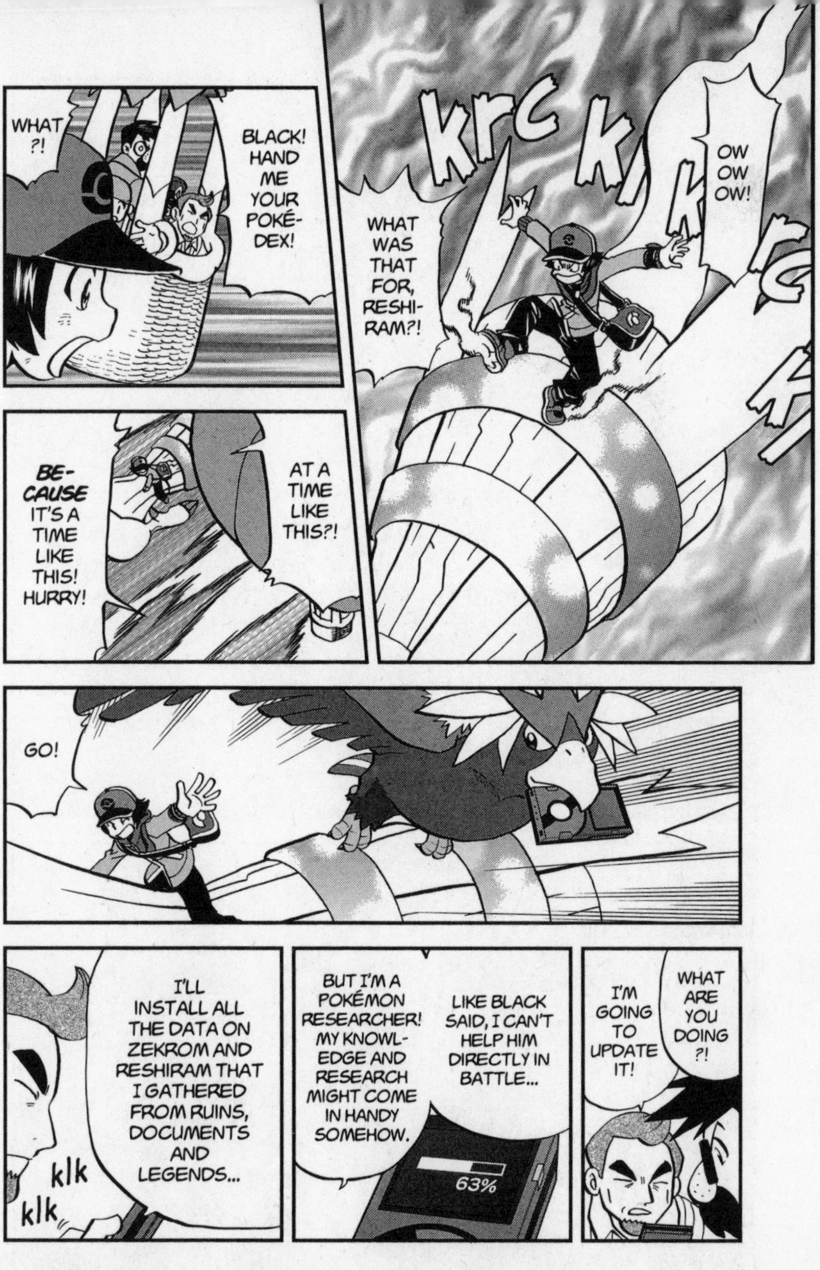
OW OW OW!
krc kik krc ki
WHAT WAS THAT FOR, RESHIRAM?!
BLACK! HAND ME YOUR POKÉDEX!
WHAT?!
AT A TIME LIKE THIS?!
BECAUSE IT'S A TIME LIKE THIS! HURRY!
GO!
WHAT ARE YOU DOING?!
I'M GOING TO UPDATE IT!
LIKE BLACK SAID, I CAN'T HELP HIM DIRECTLY IN BATTLE...
BUT I'M A POKÉMON RESEARCHER! MY KNOWLEDGE AND RESEARCH MIGHT COME IN HANDY SOMEHOW.
63%
I'LL INSTALL ALL THE DATA ON ZEKROM AND RESHIRAM THAT I GATHERED FROM RUINS, DOCUMENTS AND LEGENDS...
klk klk

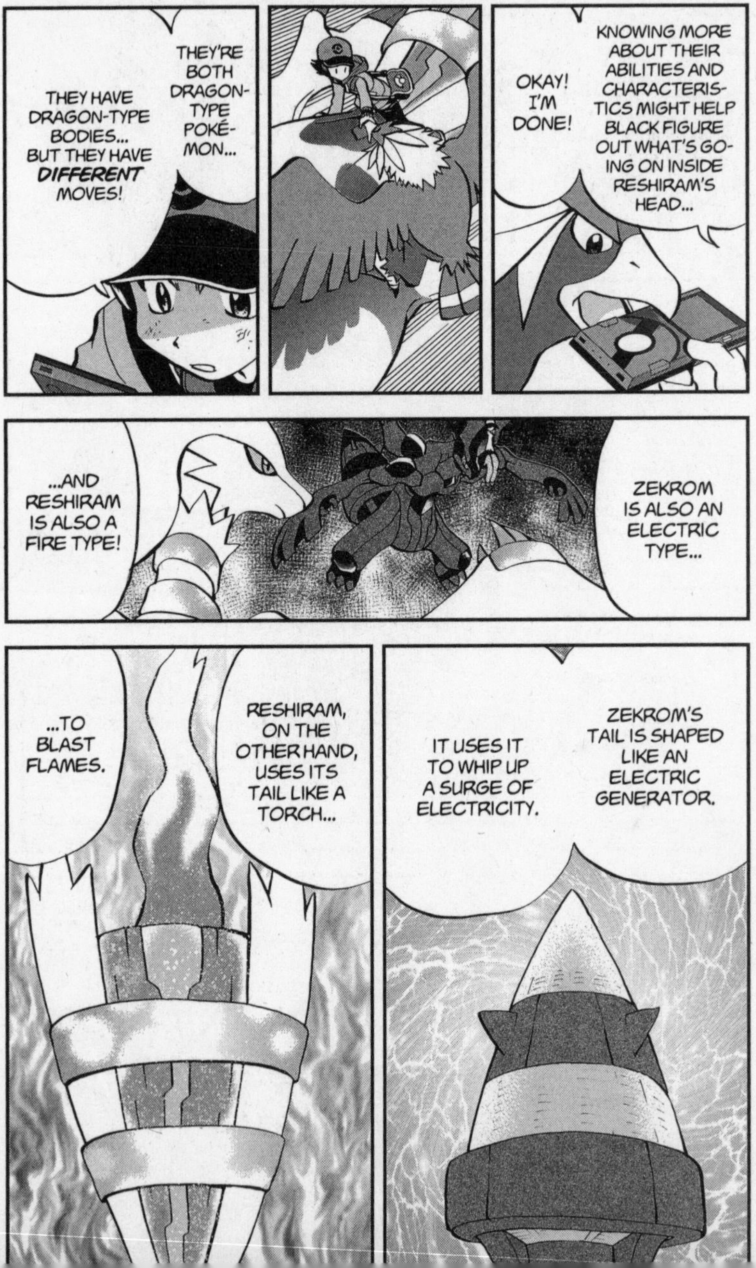
KNOWING MORE ABOUT THEIR ABILITIES AND CHARACTERIS-TICS MIGHT HELP BLACK FIGURE OUT WHAT'S GO-ING ON INSIDE RESHIRAM'S HEAD...
OKAY! I'M DONE!
THEY'RE BOTH DRAGON-TYPE POKÉ-MON...
THEY HAVE DRAGON-TYPE BODIES... BUT THEY HAVE ***DIFFERENT*** MOVES!
ZEKROM IS ALSO AN ELECTRIC TYPE...
...AND RESHIRAM IS ALSO A FIRE TYPE!
ZEKROM'S TAIL IS SHAPED LIKE AN ELECTRIC GENERATOR.
IT USES IT TO WHIP UP A SURGE OF ELECTRICITY.
RESHIRAM, ON THE OTHER HAND, USES ITS TAIL LIKE A TORCH...
...TO BLAST FLAMES.

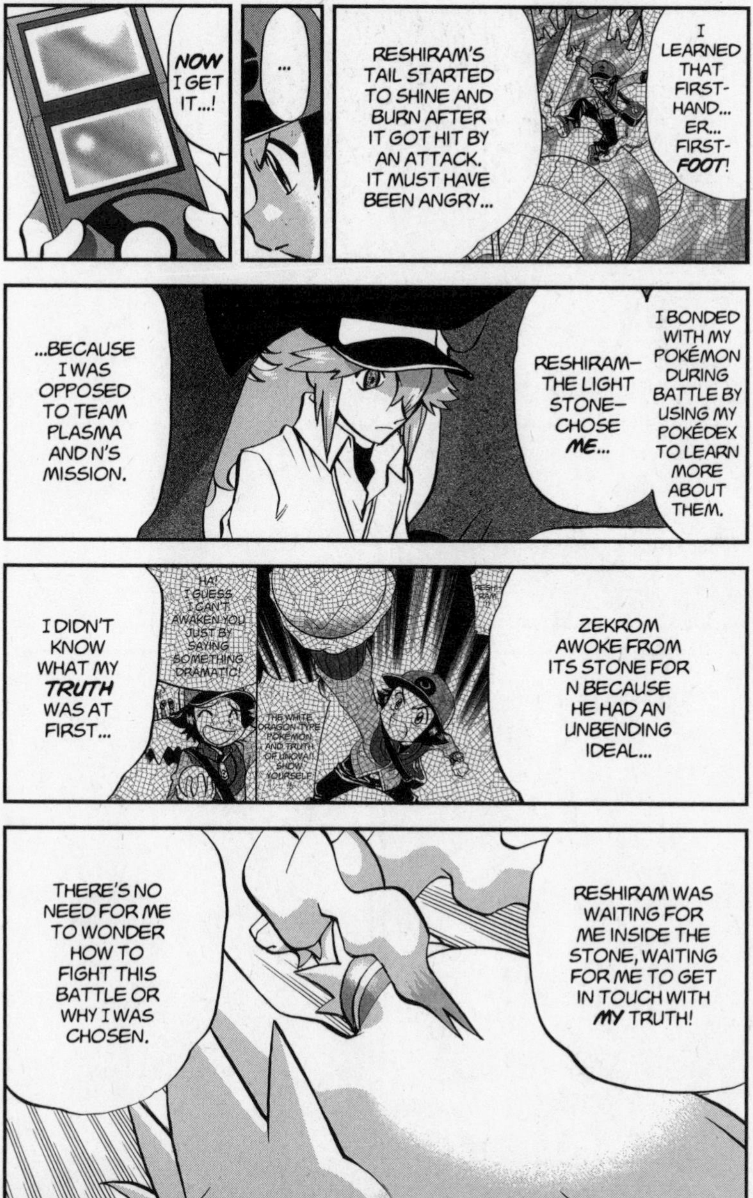
I LEARNED THAT FIRST-HAND... ER... FIRST-FOOT!
RESHIRAM'S TAIL STARTED TO SHINE AND BURN AFTER IT GOT HIT BY AN ATTACK. IT MUST HAVE BEEN ANGRY...
...
NOW I GET IT...!
I BONDED WITH MY POKÉMON DURING BATTLE BY USING MY POKÉDEX TO LEARN MORE ABOUT THEM.
RESHIRAM—THE LIGHT STONE—CHOSE ME...
...BECAUSE I WAS OPPOSED TO TEAM PLASMA AND N'S MISSION.
ZEKROM AWOKE FROM ITS STONE FOR N BECAUSE HE HAD AN UNBENDING IDEAL...
RESHI-RAM!!
THE WHITE DRAGON-TYPE POKÉMON AND TRUTH OF UNOVA!! SHOW YOURSELF!!
HA! I GUESS I CAN'T AWAKEN YOU JUST BY SAYING SOMETHING DRAMATIC!
I DIDN'T KNOW WHAT MY TRUTH WAS AT FIRST...
RESHIRAM WAS WAITING FOR ME INSIDE THE STONE, WAITING FOR ME TO GET IN TOUCH WITH MY TRUTH!
THERE'S NO NEED FOR ME TO WONDER HOW TO FIGHT THIS BATTLE OR WHY I WAS CHOSEN.

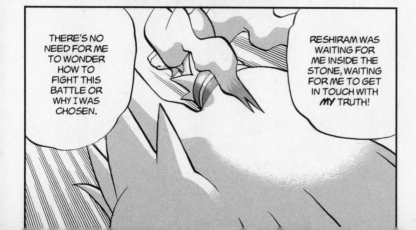

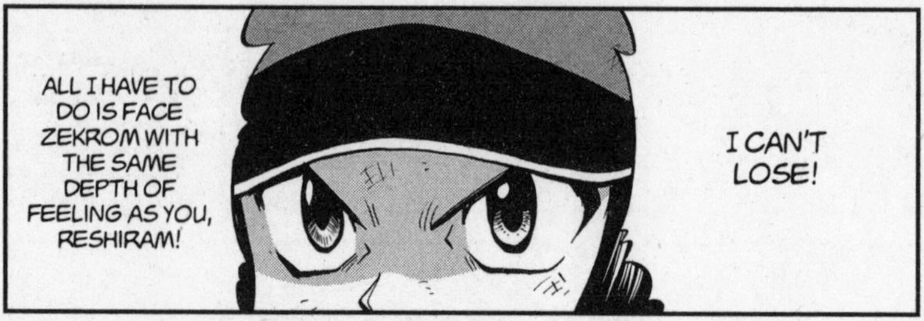
I CAN'T LOSE!
ALL I HAVE TO DO IS FACE ZEKROM WITH THE SAME DEPTH OF FEELING AS YOU, RESHIRAM!

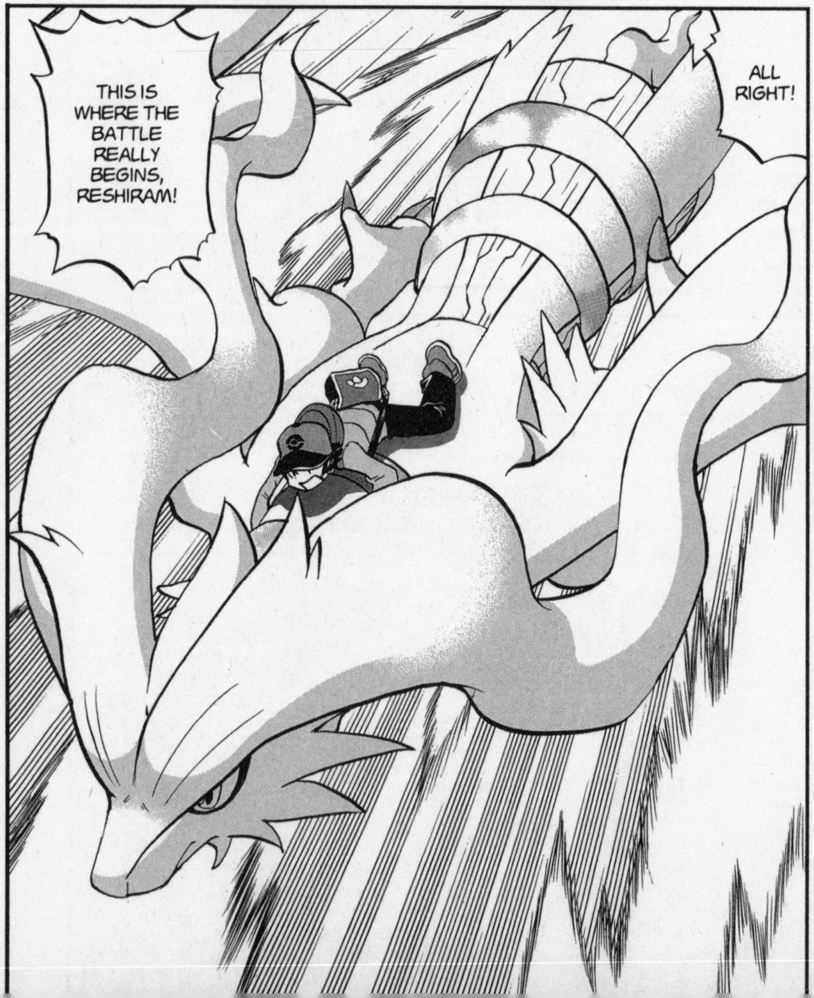
ALL RIGHT!
THIS IS WHERE THE BATTLE REALLY BEGINS, RESHIRAM!

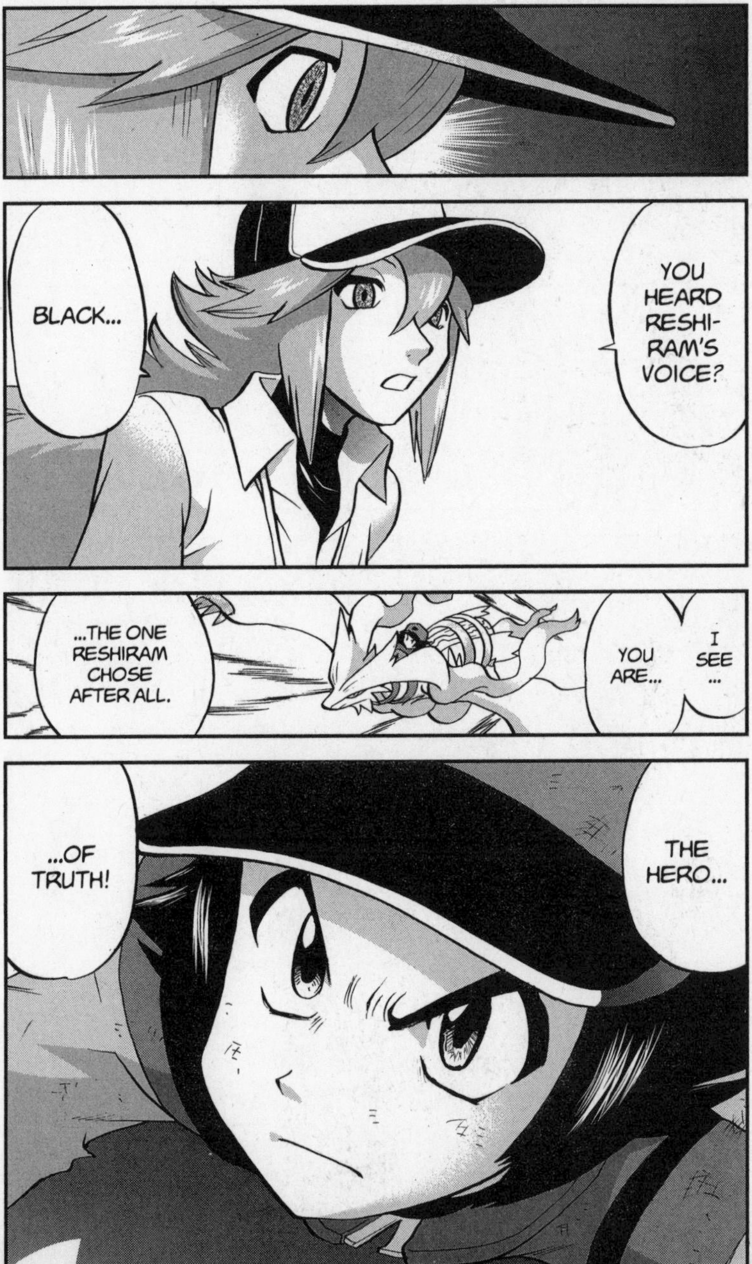
YOU HEARD RESHI-RAM'S VOICE?
BLACK...
I SEE...
YOU ARE...
...THE ONE RESHIRAM CHOSE AFTER ALL.
THE HERO...
...OF TRUTH!

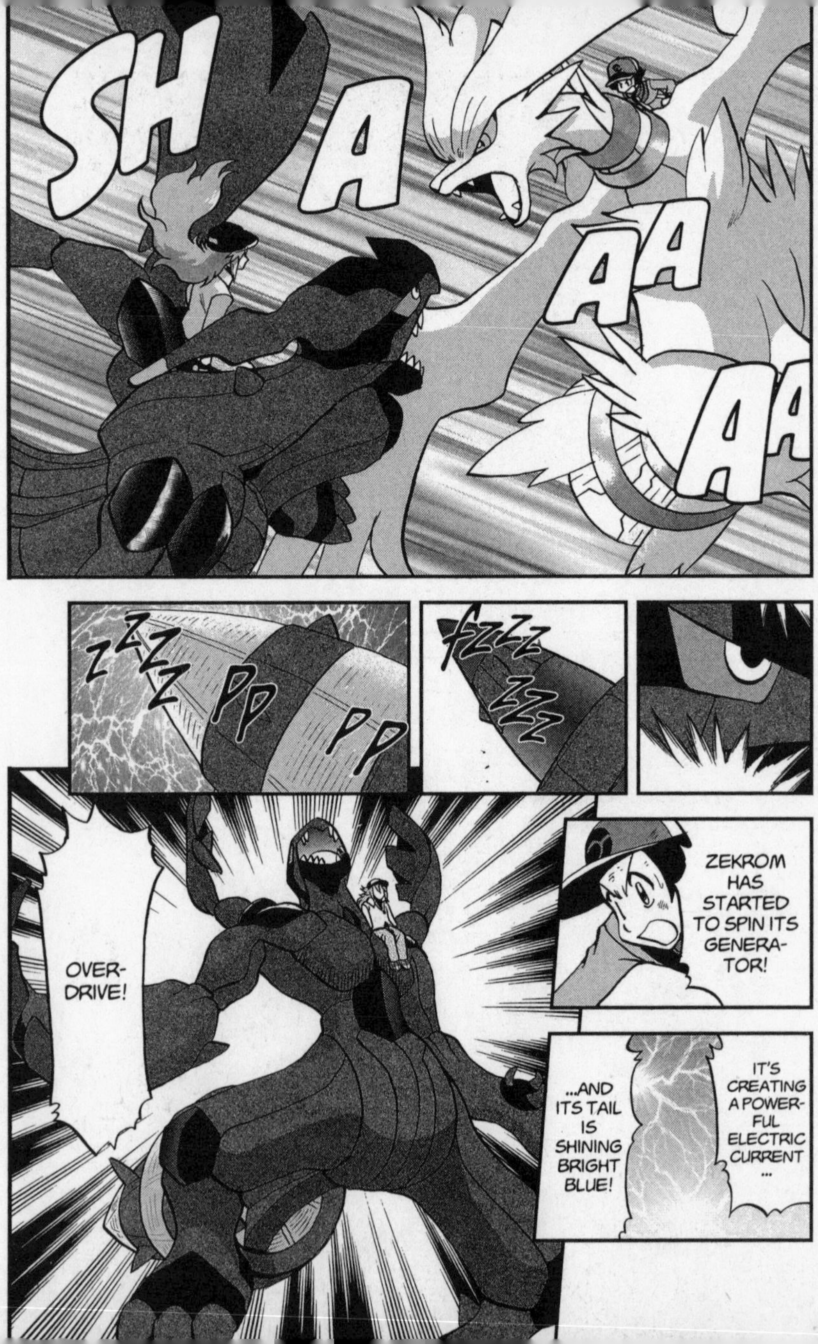
SHAAAAAA
FZZZZ ZZZ
ZZZZZ PP PP
ZEKROM HAS STARTED TO SPIN ITS GENERATOR!
IT'S CREATING A POWERFUL ELECTRIC CURRENT...
...AND ITS TAIL IS SHINING BRIGHT BLUE!
OVERDRIVE!

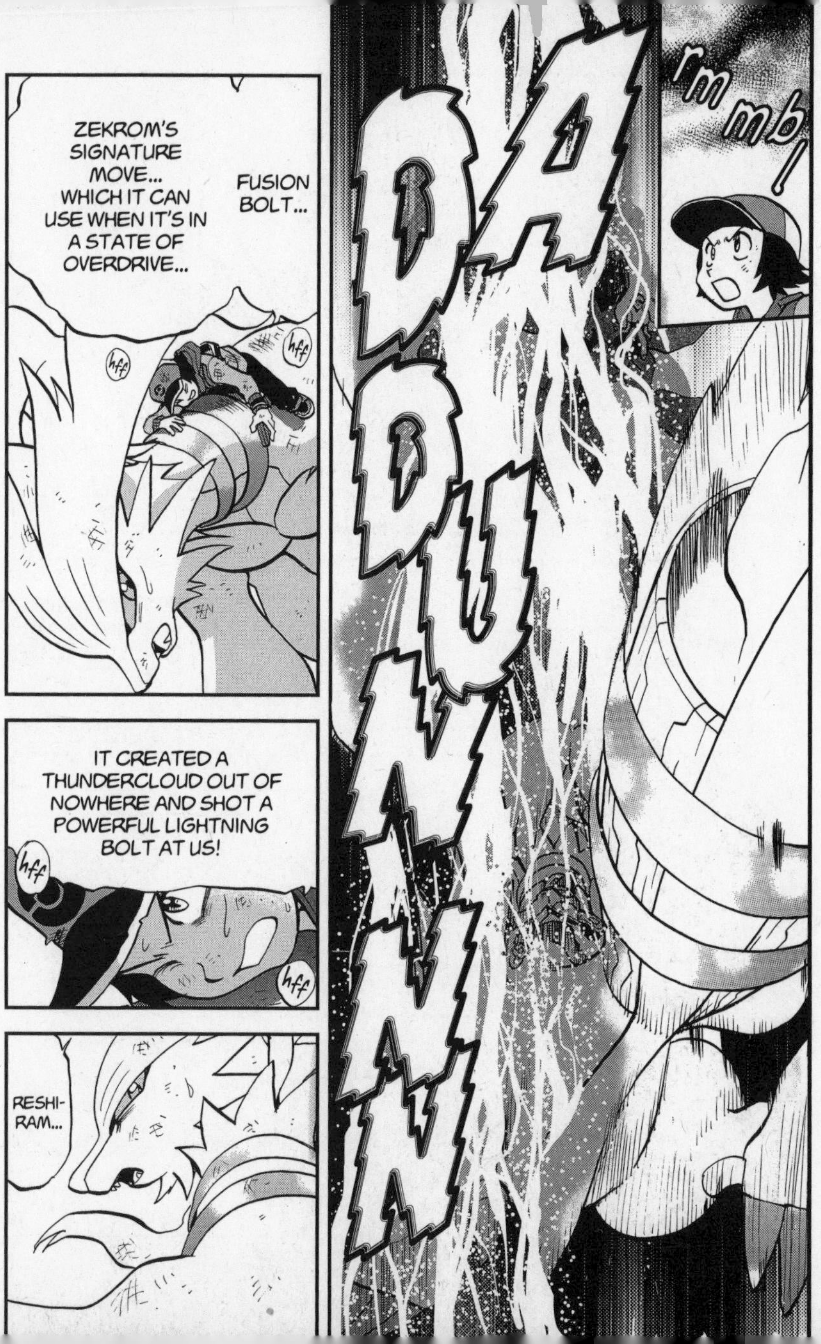
rmmbl
DADUNNN
ZEKROM'S SIGNATURE MOVE... WHICH IT CAN USE WHEN IT'S IN A STATE OF OVERDRIVE...
FUSION BOLT...
hff
hff
IT CREATED A THUNDERCLOUD OUT OF NOWHERE AND SHOT A POWERFUL LIGHTNING BOLT AT US!
hff
hff
RESHI-RAM...

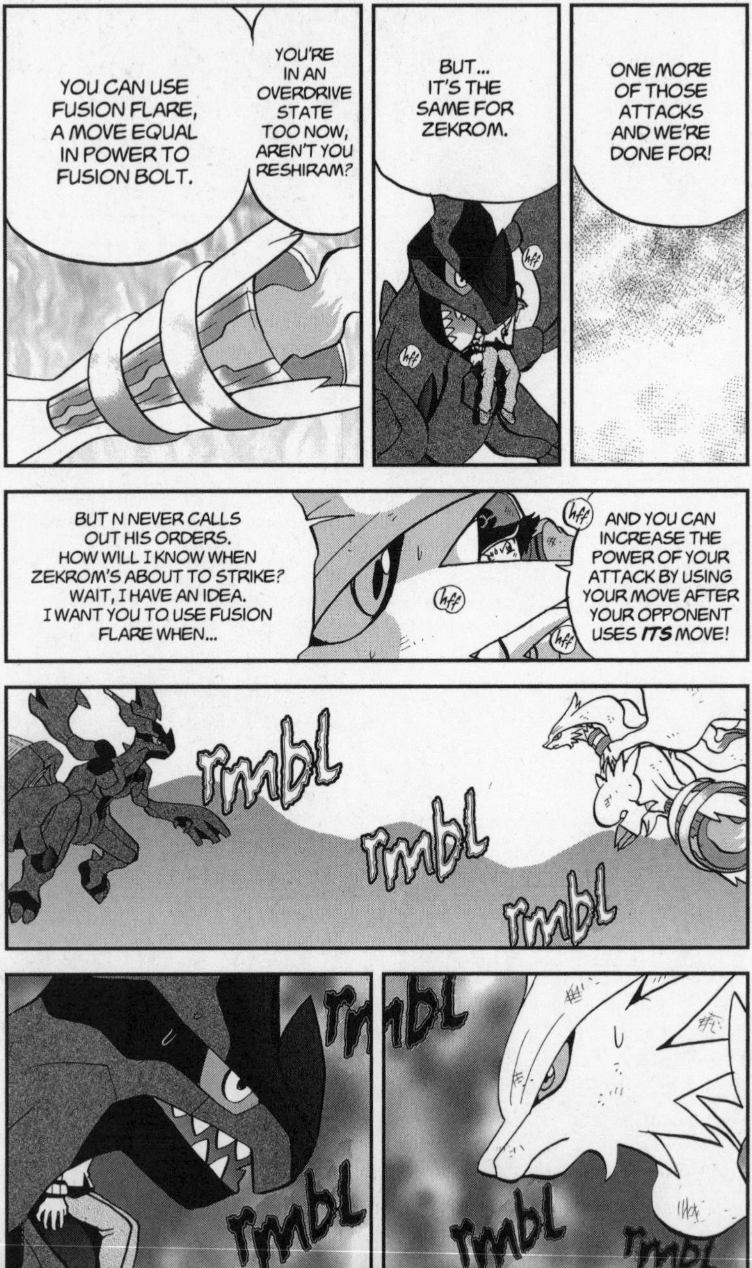
ONE MORE OF THOSE ATTACKS AND WE'RE DONE FOR!
BUT... IT'S THE SAME FOR ZEKROM.
hff
hff
YOU'RE IN AN OVERDRIVE STATE TOO NOW, AREN'T YOU RESHIRAM?
YOU CAN USE FUSION FLARE, A MOVE EQUAL IN POWER TO FUSION BOLT.
AND YOU CAN INCREASE THE POWER OF YOUR ATTACK BY USING YOUR MOVE AFTER YOUR OPPONENT USES ***ITS*** MOVE!
hff
hff
hff
hff
BUT N NEVER CALLS OUT HIS ORDERS. HOW WILL I KNOW WHEN ZEKROM'S ABOUT TO STRIKE? WAIT, I HAVE AN IDEA. I WANT YOU TO USE FUSION FLARE WHEN...
rmbl
rmbl
rmbl
rmbl
rmbl
rmbl
rmbl
rmbl

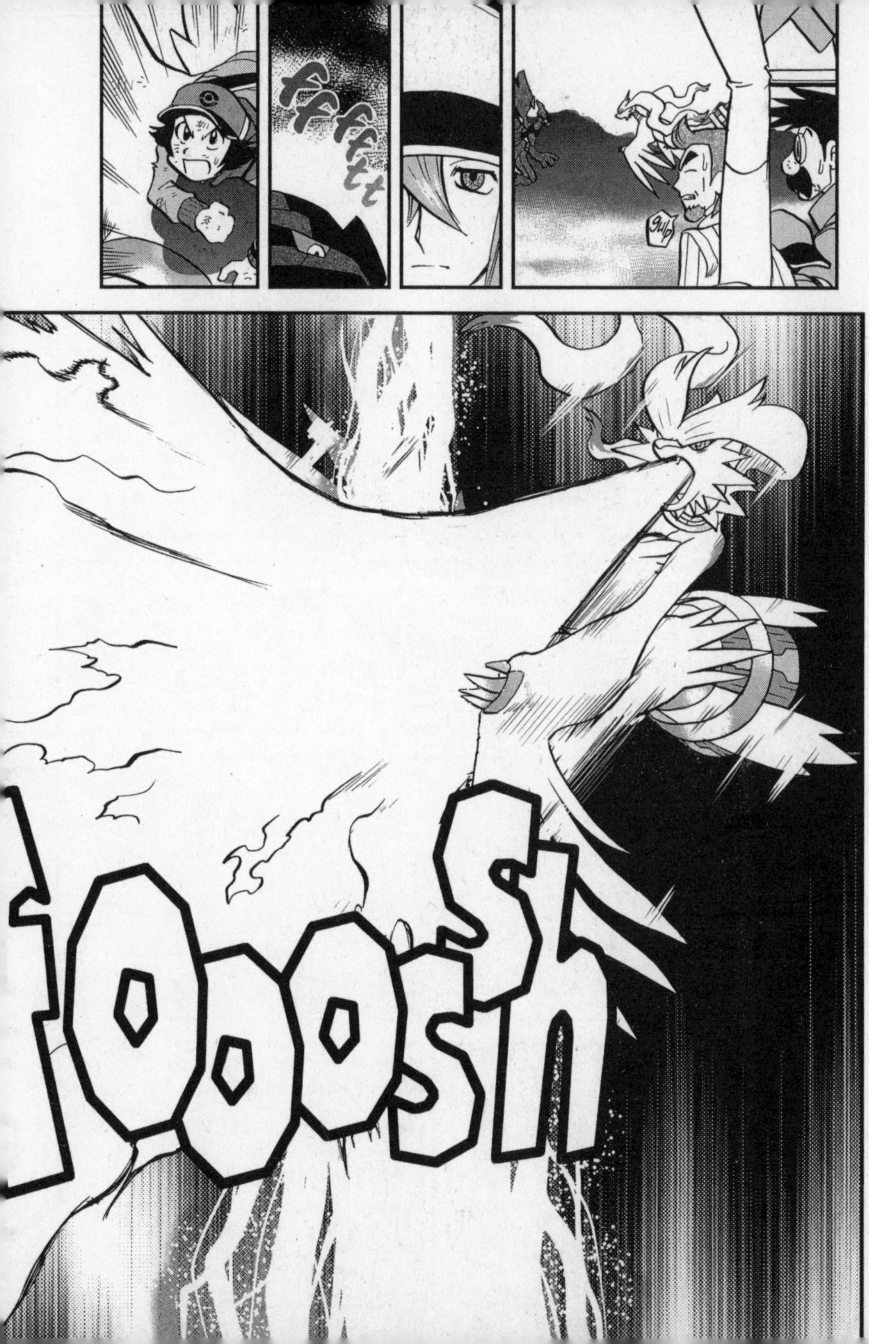
gulp
fffftt
FOOOSH

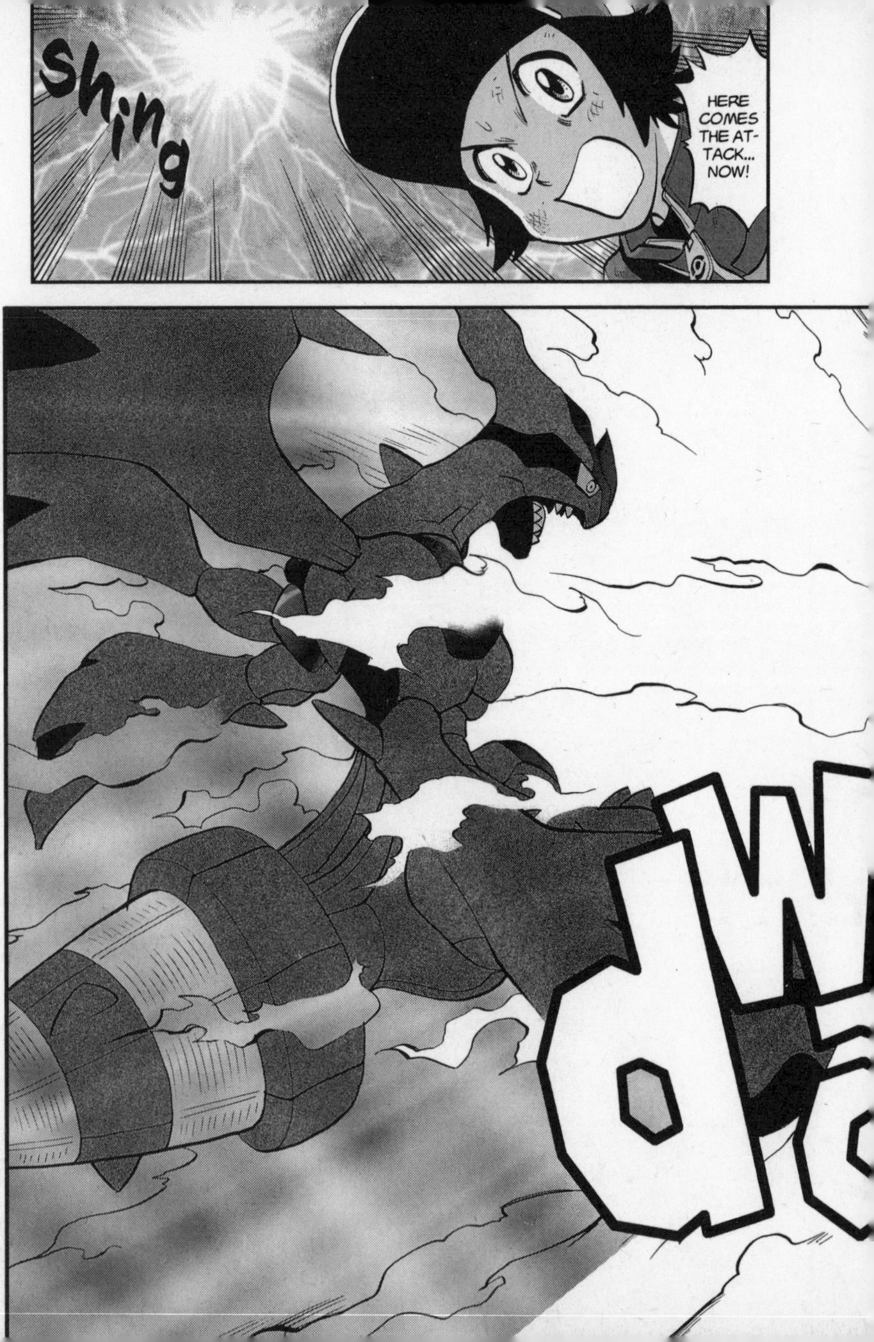
HERE COMES THE AT-TACK... NOW!
Shing

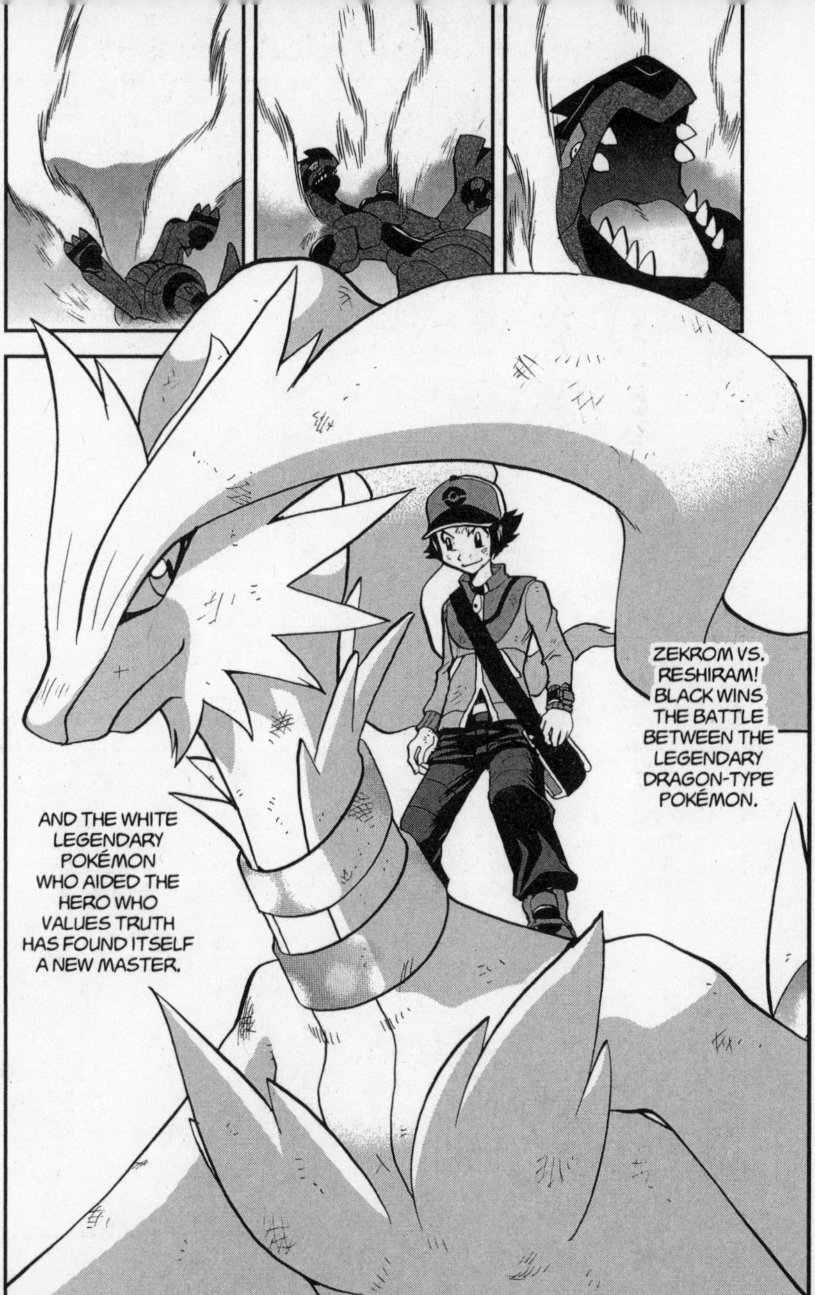
ZEKROM VS. RESHIRAM! BLACK WINS THE BATTLE BETWEEN THE LEGENDARY DRAGON-TYPE POKÉMON.
AND THE WHITE LEGENDARY POKÉMON WHO AIDED THE HERO WHO VALUES TRUTH HAS FOUND ITSELF A NEW MASTER.

Adventure ⑥⑤ What Really Matters

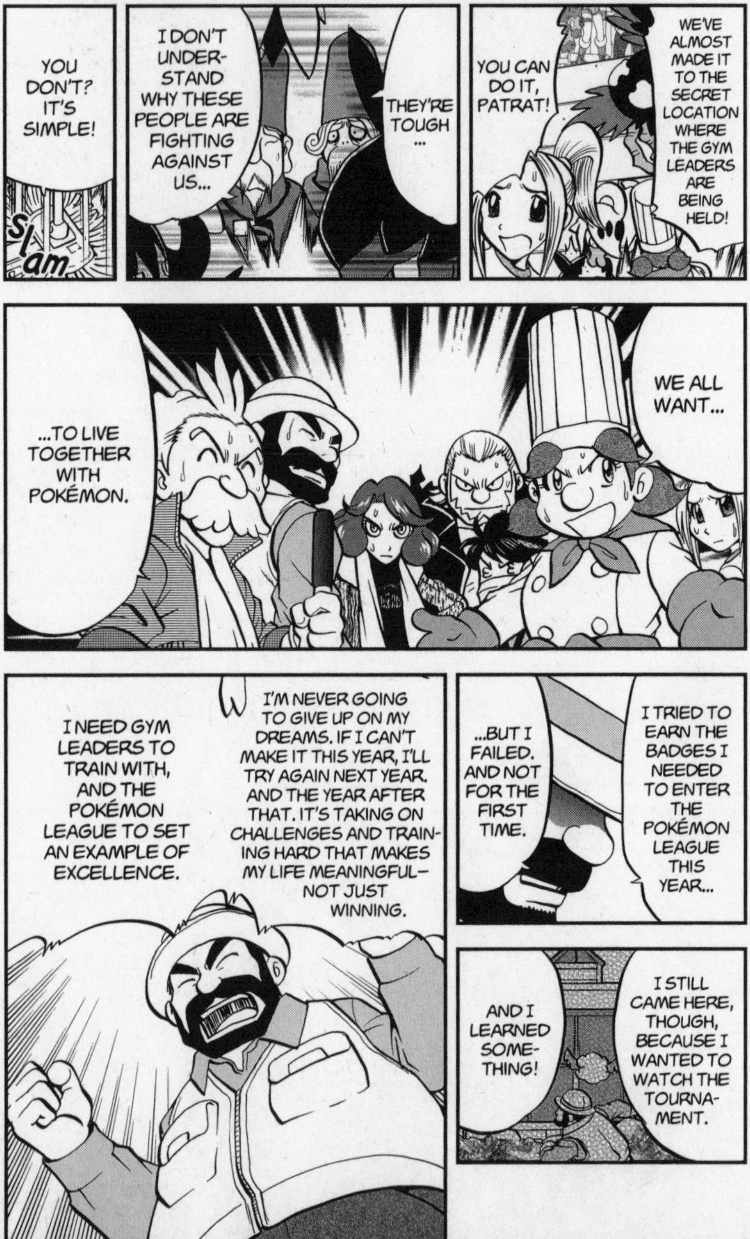
WE'VE ALMOST MADE IT TO THE SECRET LOCATION WHERE THE GYM LEADERS ARE BEING HELD!
YOU CAN DO IT, PATRAT!
THEY'RE TOUGH ...
I DON'T UNDERSTAND WHY THESE PEOPLE ARE FIGHTING AGAINST US...
YOU DON'T? IT'S SIMPLE!
Slam
WE ALL WANT...
...TO LIVE TOGETHER WITH POKÉMON.
I TRIED TO EARN THE BADGES I NEEDED TO ENTER THE POKÉMON LEAGUE THIS YEAR...
...BUT I FAILED. AND NOT FOR THE FIRST TIME.
I STILL CAME HERE, THOUGH, BECAUSE I WANTED TO WATCH THE TOURNAMENT.
AND I LEARNED SOMETHING!
I'M NEVER GOING TO GIVE UP ON MY DREAMS. IF I CAN'T MAKE IT THIS YEAR, I'LL TRY AGAIN NEXT YEAR. AND THE YEAR AFTER THAT. IT'S TAKING ON CHALLENGES AND TRAINING HARD THAT MAKES MY LIFE MEANINGFUL—NOT JUST WINNING.
I NEED GYM LEADERS TO TRAIN WITH, AND THE POKÉMON LEAGUE TO SET AN EXAMPLE OF EXCELLENCE.

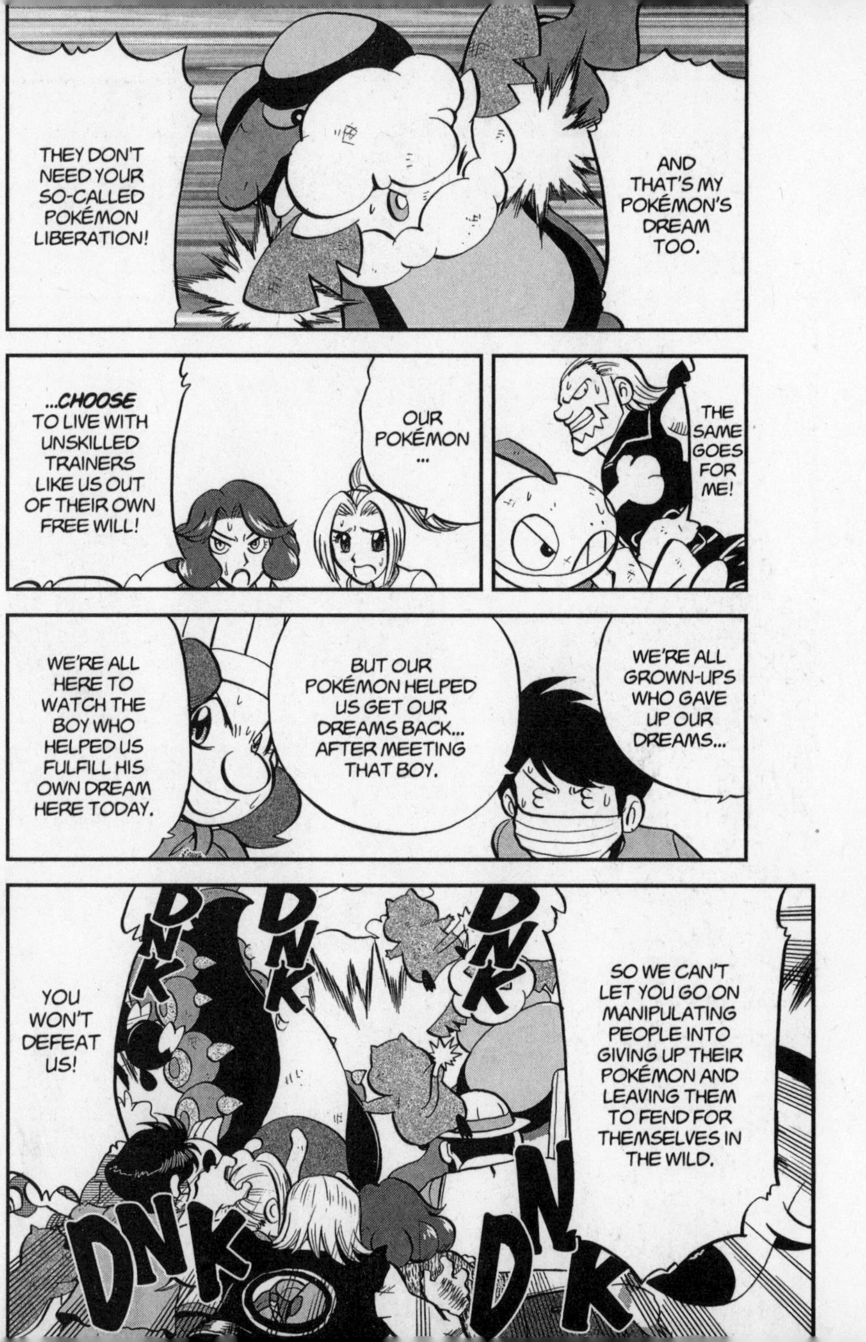
AND THAT'S MY POKÉMON'S DREAM TOO.
THEY DON'T NEED YOUR SO-CALLED POKÉMON LIBERATION!
THE SAME GOES FOR ME!
OUR POKÉMON ...
...*CHOOSE* TO LIVE WITH UNSKILLED TRAINERS LIKE US OUT OF THEIR OWN FREE WILL!
WE'RE ALL GROWN-UPS WHO GAVE UP OUR DREAMS...
BUT OUR POKÉMON HELPED US GET OUR DREAMS BACK... AFTER MEETING THAT BOY.
WE'RE ALL HERE TO WATCH THE BOY WHO HELPED US FULFILL HIS OWN DREAM HERE TODAY.
SO WE CAN'T LET YOU GO ON MANIPULATING PEOPLE INTO GIVING UP THEIR POKÉMON AND LEAVING THEM TO FEND FOR THEMSELVES IN THE WILD.
DNK
DNK
DNK
YOU WON'T DEFEAT US!
DNK
DNK

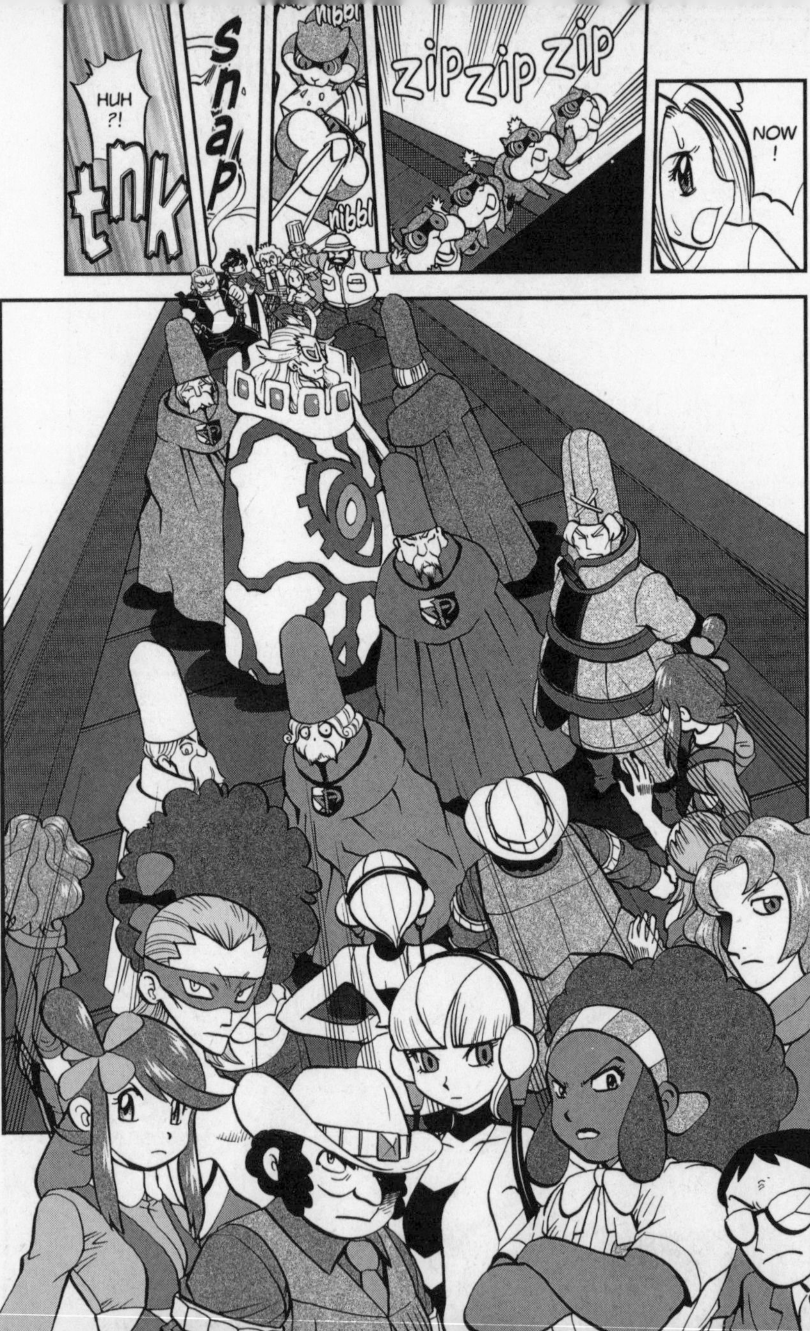
NOW !
zip zip zip
nibbl
nibbl
snap
HUH ?!
tnk

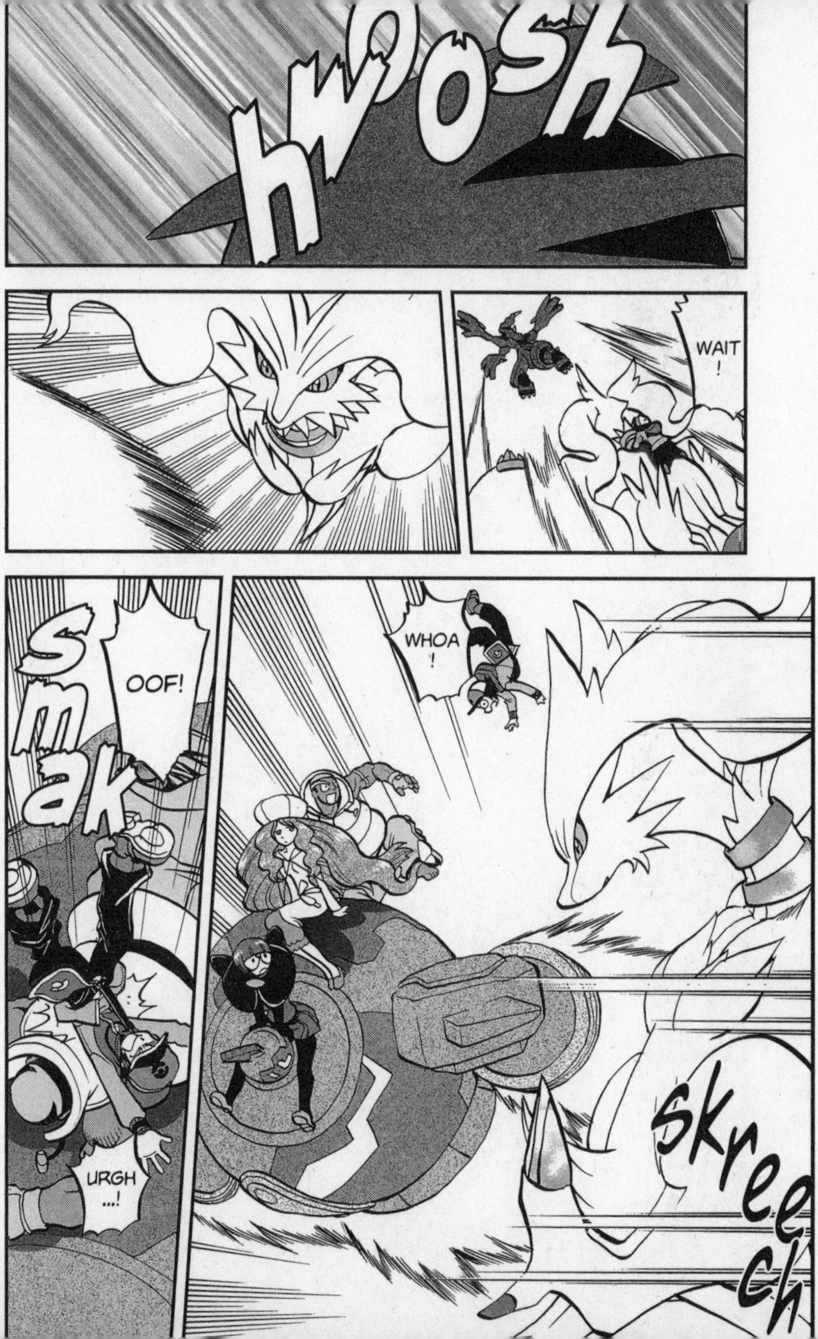
hwoosh
WAIT!
WHOA!
skreech
OOF!
smak
URGH ...!

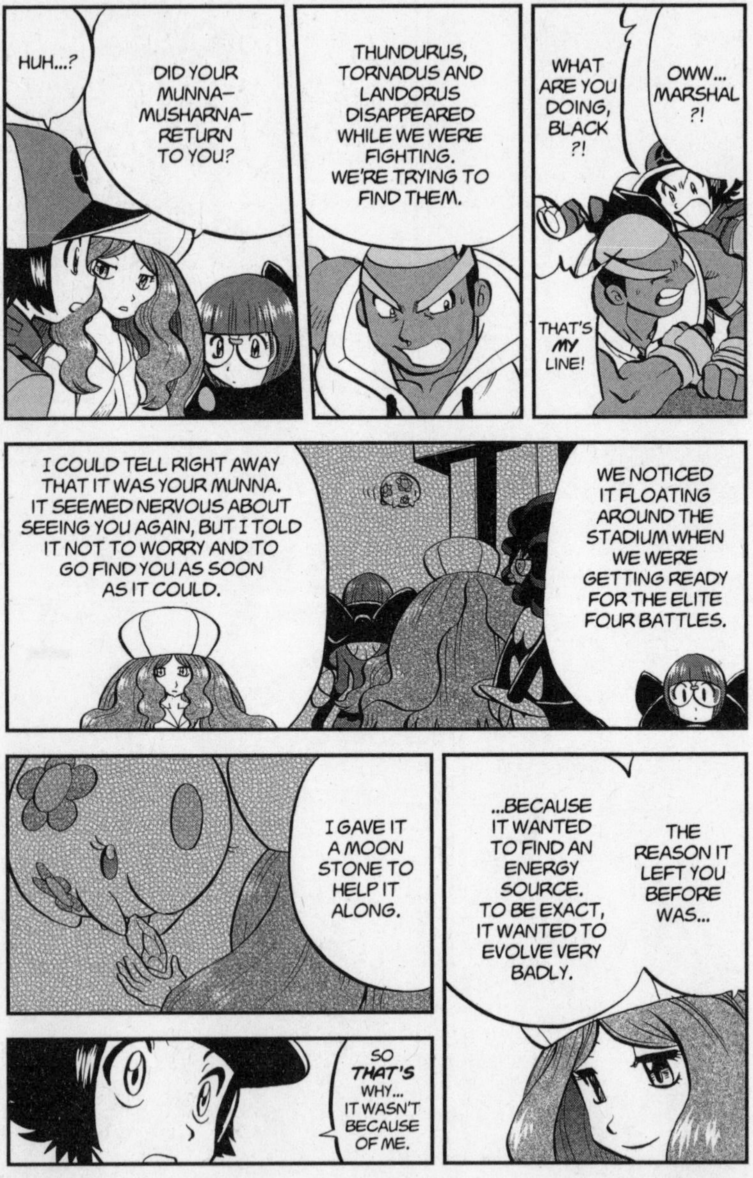
OWW... MARSHAL ?!
WHAT ARE YOU DOING, BLACK ?!
THAT'S *MY* LINE!
THUNDURUS, TORNADUS AND LANDORUS DISAPPEARED WHILE WE WERE FIGHTING. WE'RE TRYING TO FIND THEM.
HUH...?
DID YOUR MUNNA-MUSHARNA-RETURN TO YOU?
WE NOTICED IT FLOATING AROUND THE STADIUM WHEN WE WERE GETTING READY FOR THE ELITE FOUR BATTLES.
I COULD TELL RIGHT AWAY THAT IT WAS YOUR MUNNA. IT SEEMED NERVOUS ABOUT SEEING YOU AGAIN, BUT I TOLD IT NOT TO WORRY AND TO GO FIND YOU AS SOON AS IT COULD.
THE REASON IT LEFT YOU BEFORE WAS...
...BECAUSE IT WANTED TO FIND AN ENERGY SOURCE. TO BE EXACT, IT WANTED TO EVOLVE VERY BADLY.
I GAVE IT A MOON STONE TO HELP IT ALONG.
SO ***THAT'S*** WHY... IT WASN'T BECAUSE OF ME.

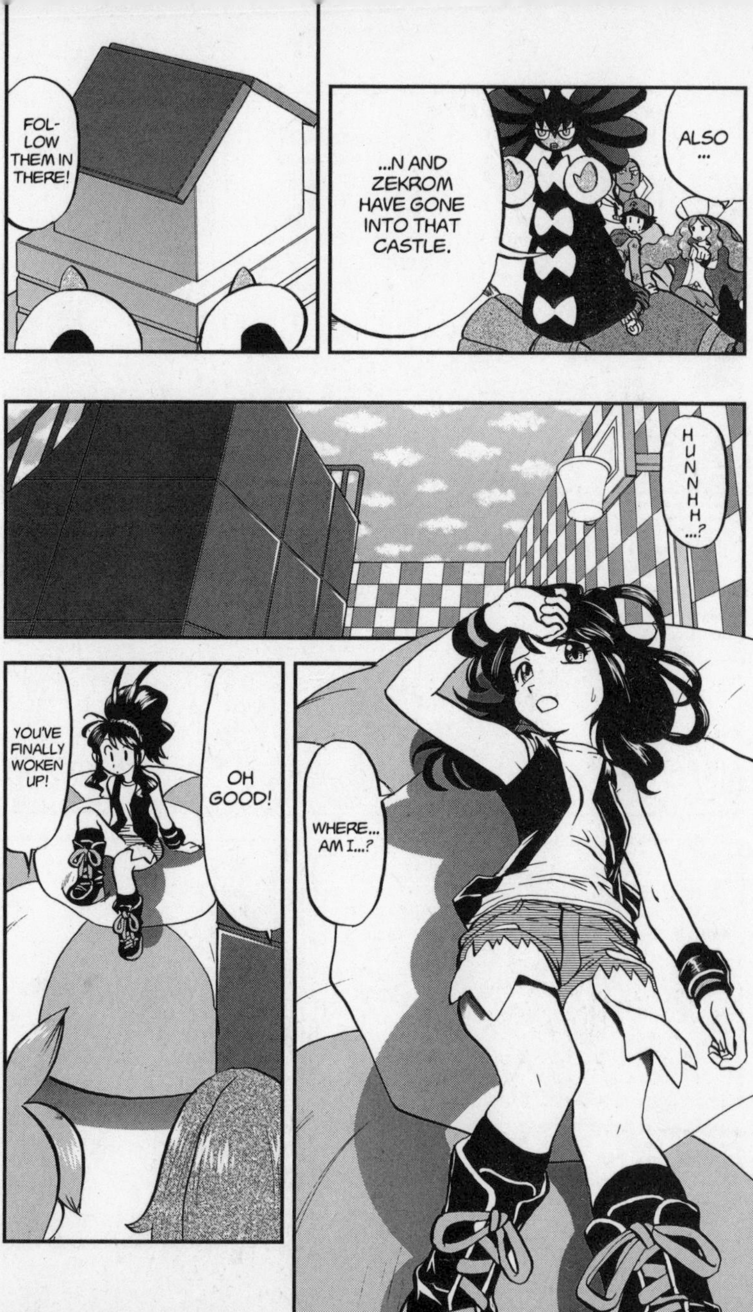
ALSO ...
...N AND ZEKROM HAVE GONE INTO THAT CASTLE.
FOL-LOW THEM IN THERE!
HUNNHH ...?
WHERE... AM I...?
OH GOOD!
YOU'VE FINALLY WOKEN UP!

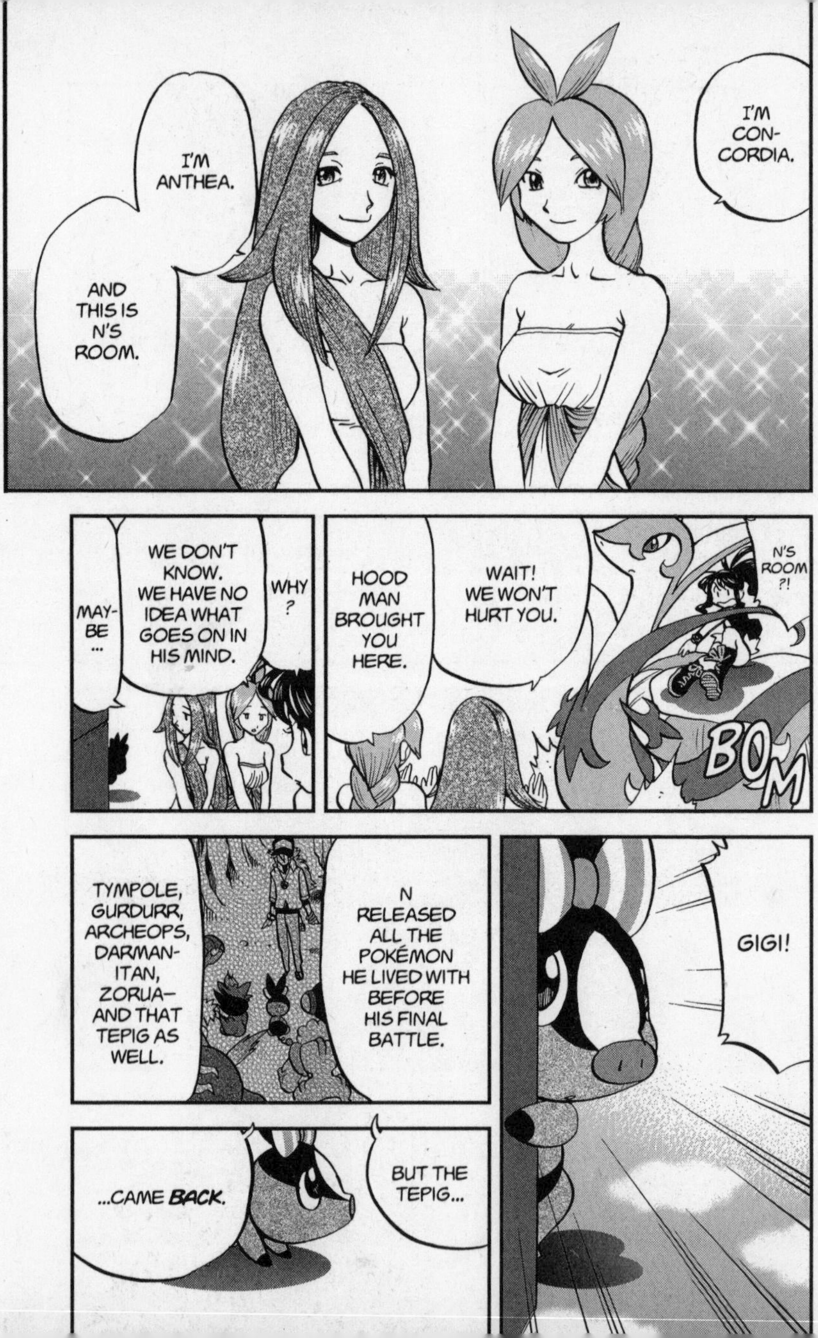
I'M CON-CORDIA.
I'M ANTHEA.
AND THIS IS N'S ROOM.
N'S ROOM ?!
WAIT! WE WON'T HURT YOU.
HOOD MAN BROUGHT YOU HERE.
BOM
WHY?
WE DON'T KNOW. WE HAVE NO IDEA WHAT GOES ON IN HIS MIND.
MAY-BE ...
GIGI!
N RELEASED ALL THE POKÉMON HE LIVED WITH BEFORE HIS FINAL BATTLE.
TYMPOLE, GURDURR, ARCHEOPS, DARMAN-ITAN, ZORUA— AND THAT TEPIG AS WELL.
BUT THE TEPIG...
...CAME **BACK**.

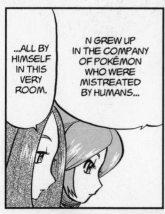

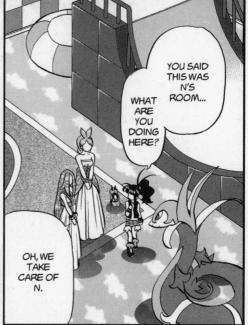

YOU SAID THIS WAS N'S ROOM...
WHAT ARE YOU DOING HERE?
OH, WE TAKE CARE OF N.
N GREW UP IN THE COMPANY OF POKÉMON WHO WERE MISTREATED BY HUMANS...
...ALL BY HIMSELF IN THIS VERY ROOM.
WHAT?!
SINCE HE WAS A SMALL CHILD, N HAS HAD THE SPECIAL ABILITY TO HEAR THE VOICES OF POKÉMON.
HE HAD NO FAMILY AND PEOPLE THOUGHT HE WAS CRAZY...
SO GHETSIS ...
...TOOK N IN.
GHETSIS ADOPT-ED...
...N AS HIS SON.

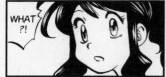

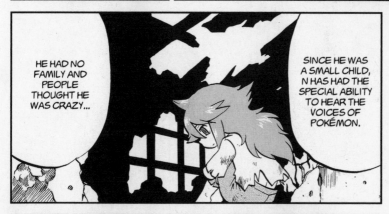

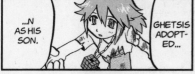

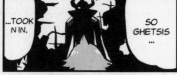

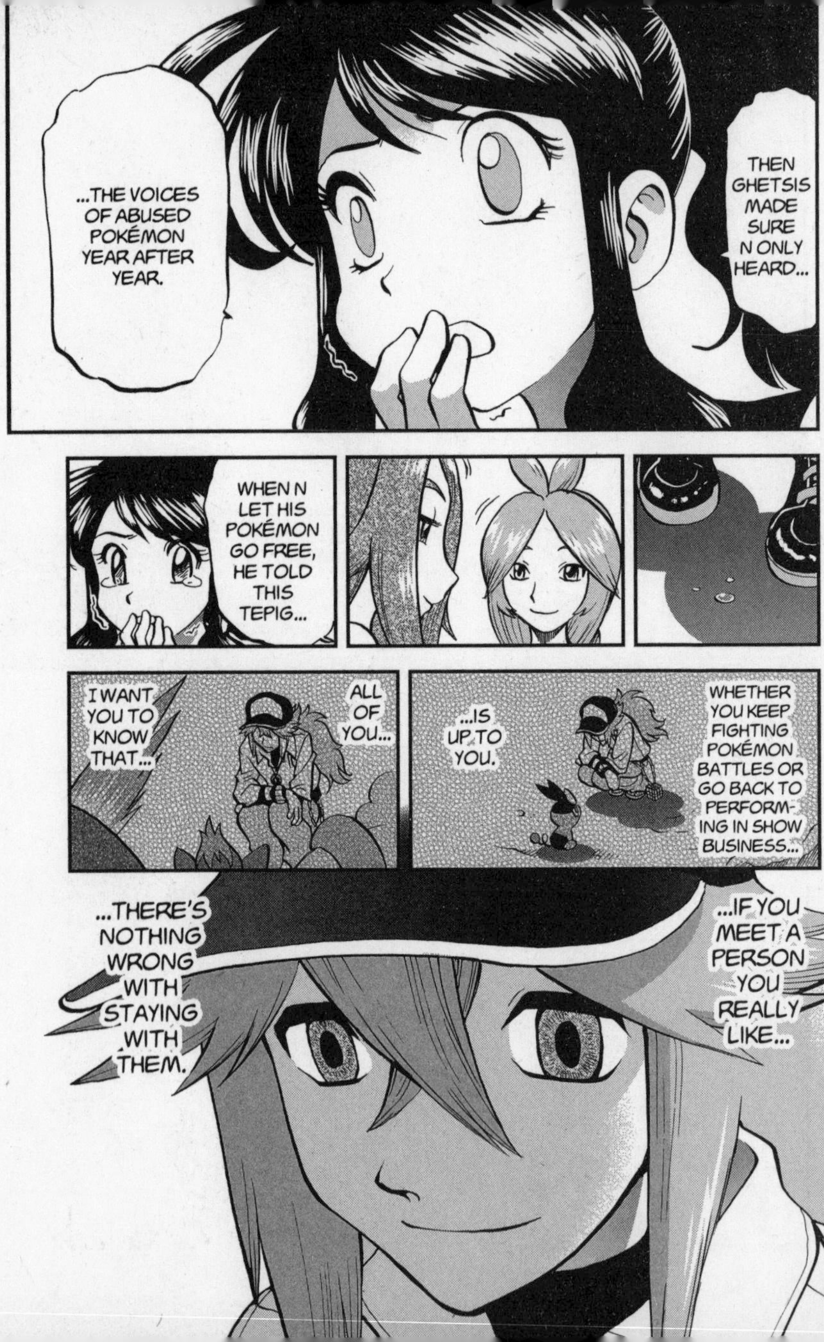
THEN GHETSIS MADE SURE N ONLY HEARD...
...THE VOICES OF ABUSED POKÉMON YEAR AFTER YEAR.
WHEN N LET HIS POKÉMON GO FREE, HE TOLD THIS TEPIG...
WHETHER YOU KEEP FIGHTING POKÉMON BATTLES OR GO BACK TO PERFORMING IN SHOW BUSINESS...
...IS UP TO YOU.
ALL OF YOU...
I WANT YOU TO KNOW THAT...
...IF YOU MEET A PERSON YOU REALLY LIKE...
...THERE'S NOTHING WRONG WITH STAYING WITH THEM.

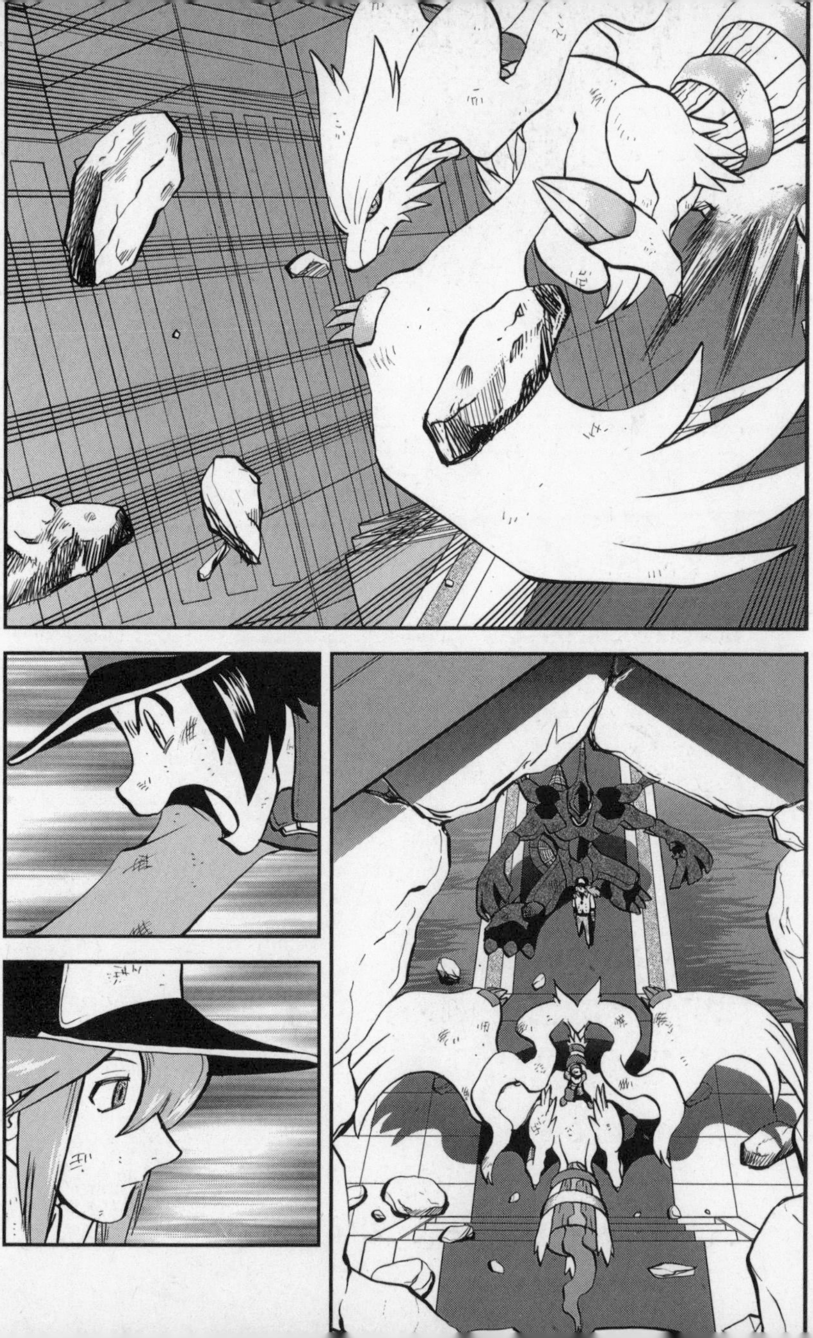

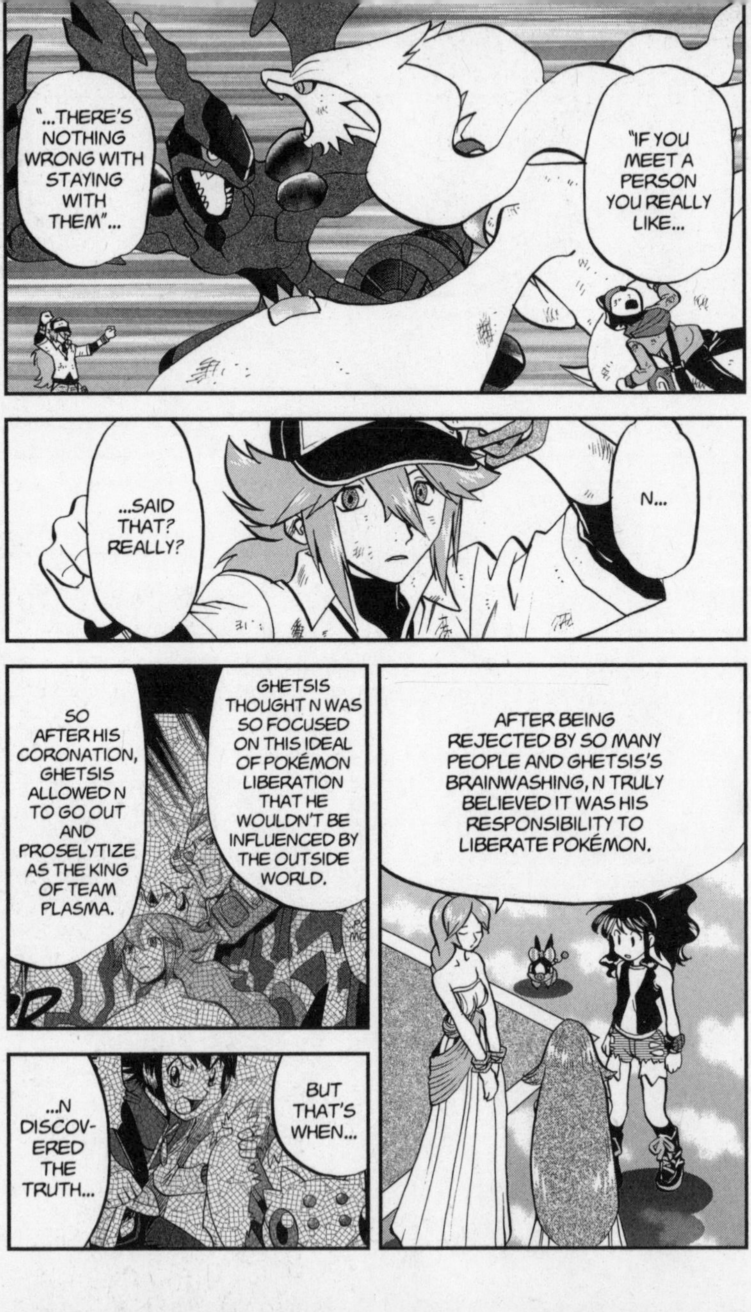
"IF YOU MEET A PERSON YOU REALLY LIKE...
"...THERE'S NOTHING WRONG WITH STAYING WITH THEM"...
N...
...SAID THAT? REALLY?
AFTER BEING REJECTED BY SO MANY PEOPLE AND GHETSIS'S BRAINWASHING, N TRULY BELIEVED IT WAS HIS RESPONSIBILITY TO LIBERATE POKÉMON.
GHETSIS THOUGHT N WAS SO FOCUSED ON THIS IDEAL OF POKÉMON LIBERATION THAT HE WOULDN'T BE INFLUENCED BY THE OUTSIDE WORLD.
SO AFTER HIS CORONATION, GHETSIS ALLOWED N TO GO OUT AND PROSELYTIZE AS THE KING OF TEAM PLASMA.
BUT THAT'S WHEN...
...N DISCOVERED THE TRUTH...

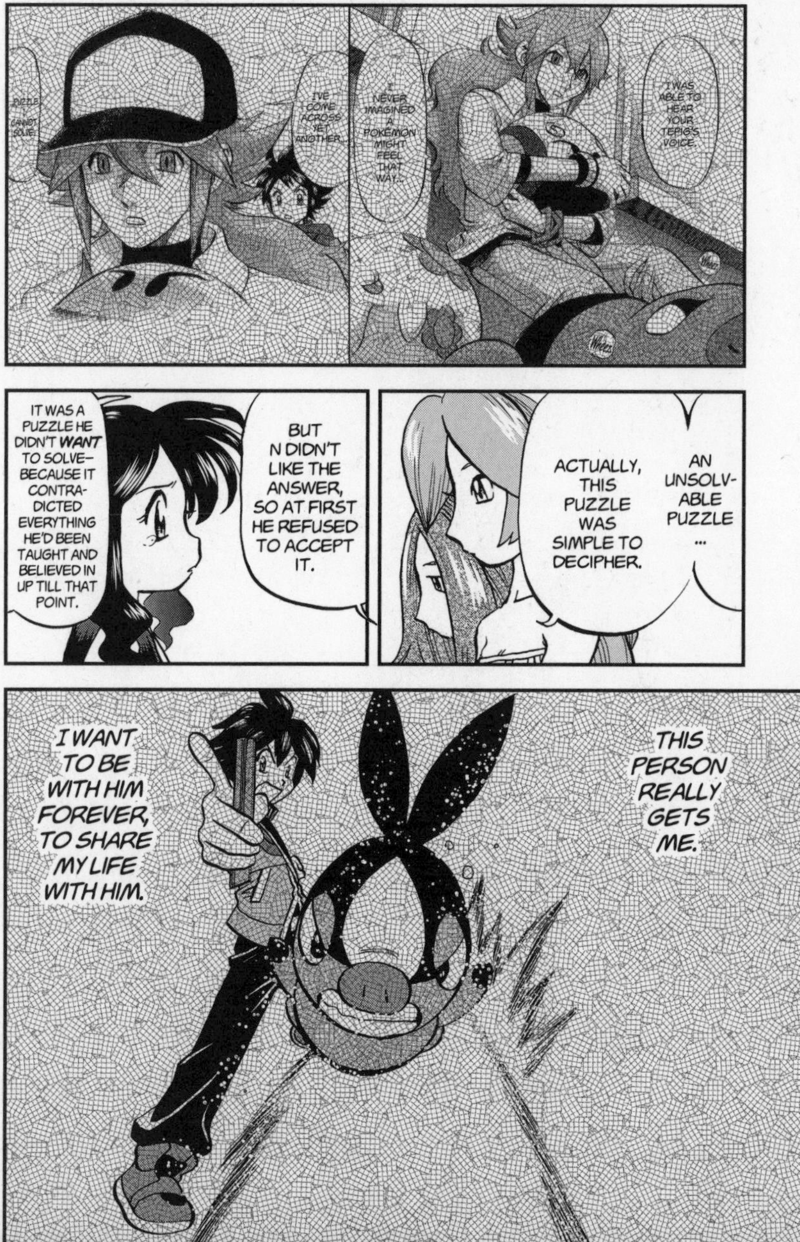
I WAS ABLE TO HEAR YOUR TEPIG'S VOICE.
I NEVER IMAGINED A POKÉMON MIGHT FEEL THAT WAY...
I'VE COME ACROSS YET ANOTHER...
PUZZLE I CANNOT SOLVE.
AN UNSOLVABLE PUZZLE...
ACTUALLY, THIS PUZZLE WAS SIMPLE TO DECIPHER.
BUT N DIDN'T LIKE THE ANSWER, SO AT FIRST HE REFUSED TO ACCEPT IT.
IT WAS A PUZZLE HE DIDN'T *WANT* TO SOLVE—BECAUSE IT CONTRADICTED EVERYTHING HE'D BEEN TAUGHT AND BELIEVED IN UP TILL THAT POINT.
THIS PERSON REALLY GETS ME.
I WANT TO BE WITH HIM FOREVER, TO SHARE MY LIFE WITH HIM.

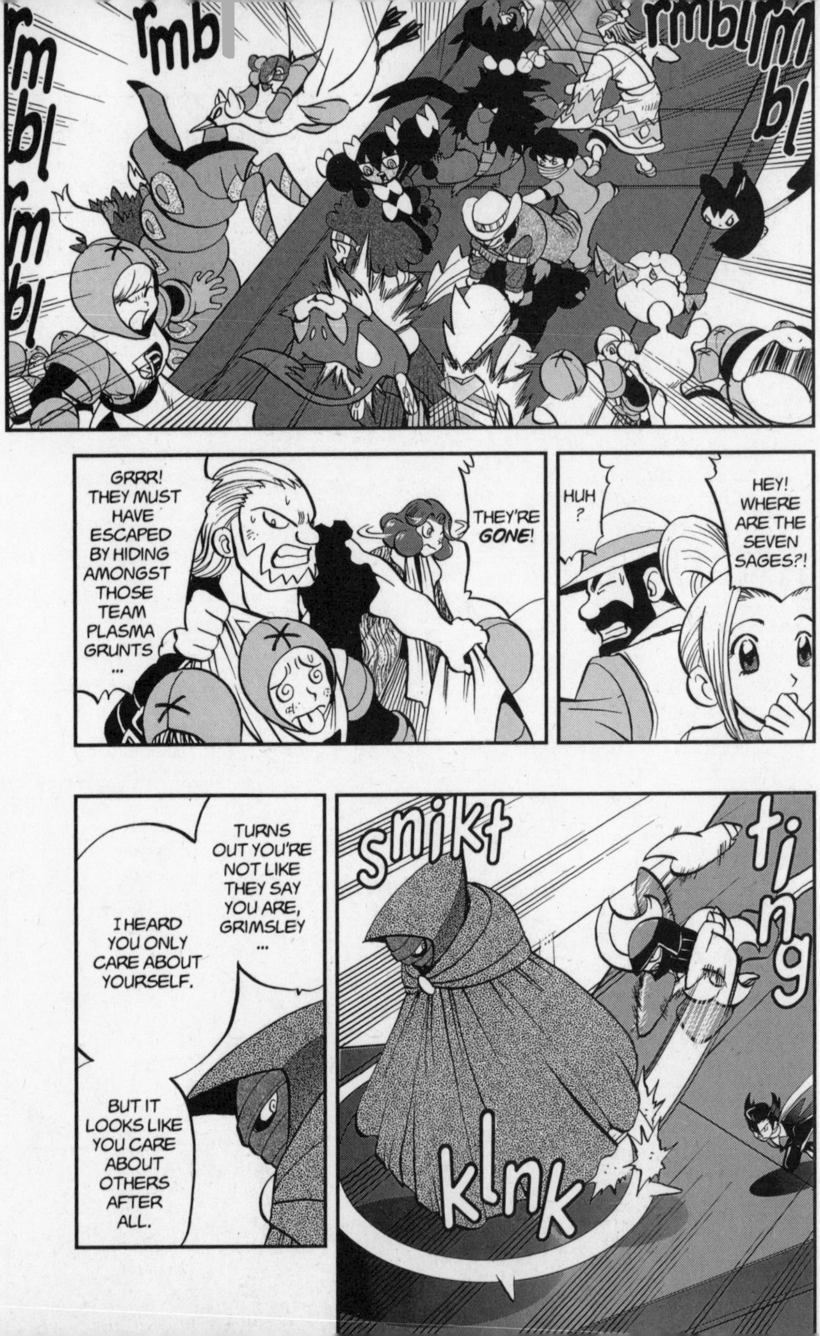
rmblrmbl
rmb
rmblrmbl
HEY! WHERE ARE THE SEVEN SAGES?!
HUH?
THEY'RE *GONE*!
GRRR! THEY MUST HAVE ESCAPED BY HIDING AMONGST THOSE TEAM PLASMA GRUNTS...
snikt
ting
klink
TURNS OUT YOU'RE NOT LIKE THEY SAY YOU ARE, GRIMSLEY...
I HEARD YOU ONLY CARE ABOUT YOURSELF.
BUT IT LOOKS LIKE YOU CARE ABOUT OTHERS AFTER ALL.

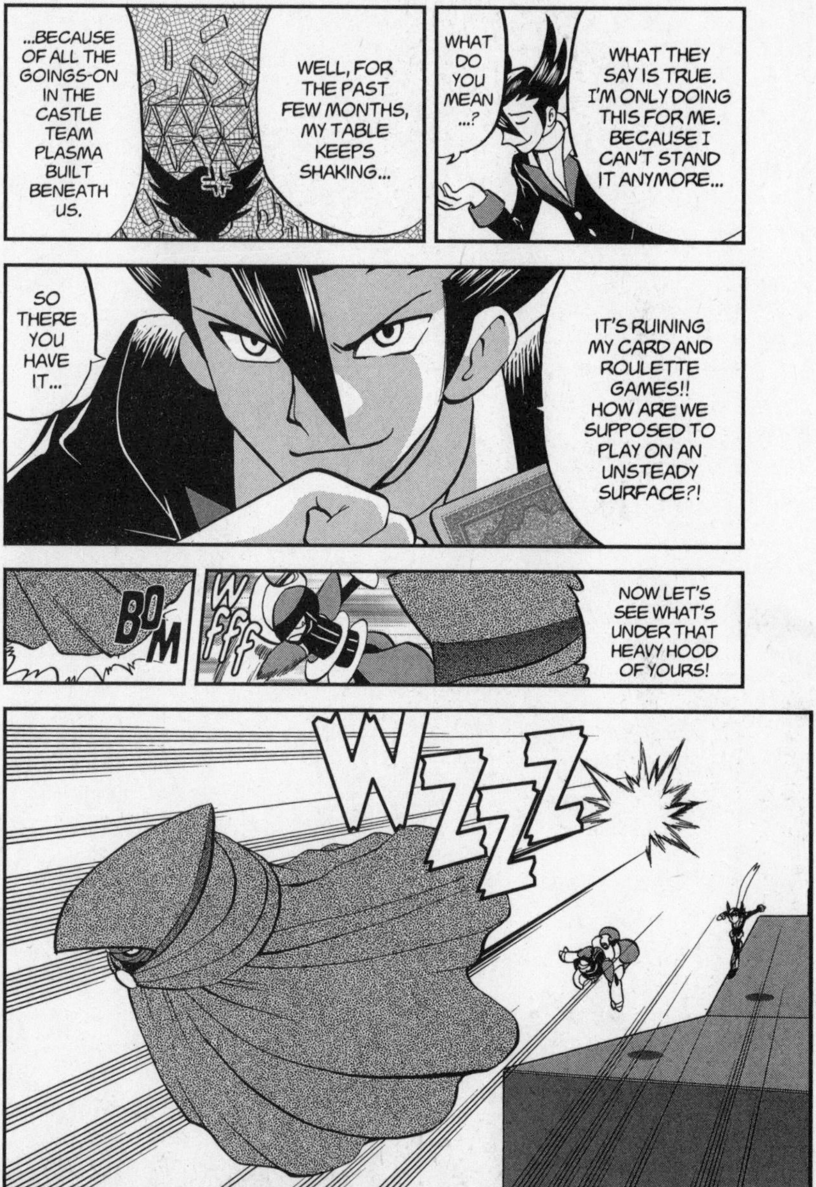
WHAT THEY SAY IS TRUE. I'M ONLY DOING THIS FOR ME. BECAUSE I CAN'T STAND IT ANYMORE...
WHAT DO YOU MEAN ...?
WELL, FOR THE PAST FEW MONTHS, MY TABLE KEEPS SHAKING...
...BECAUSE OF ALL THE GOINGS-ON IN THE CASTLE TEAM PLASMA BUILT BENEATH US.
IT'S RUINING MY CARD AND ROULETTE GAMES!! HOW ARE WE SUPPOSED TO PLAY ON AN UNSTEADY SURFACE?!
SO THERE YOU HAVE IT...
NOW LET'S SEE WHAT'S UNDER THAT HEAVY HOOD OF YOURS!
WFFF
BOOM
WZZZ

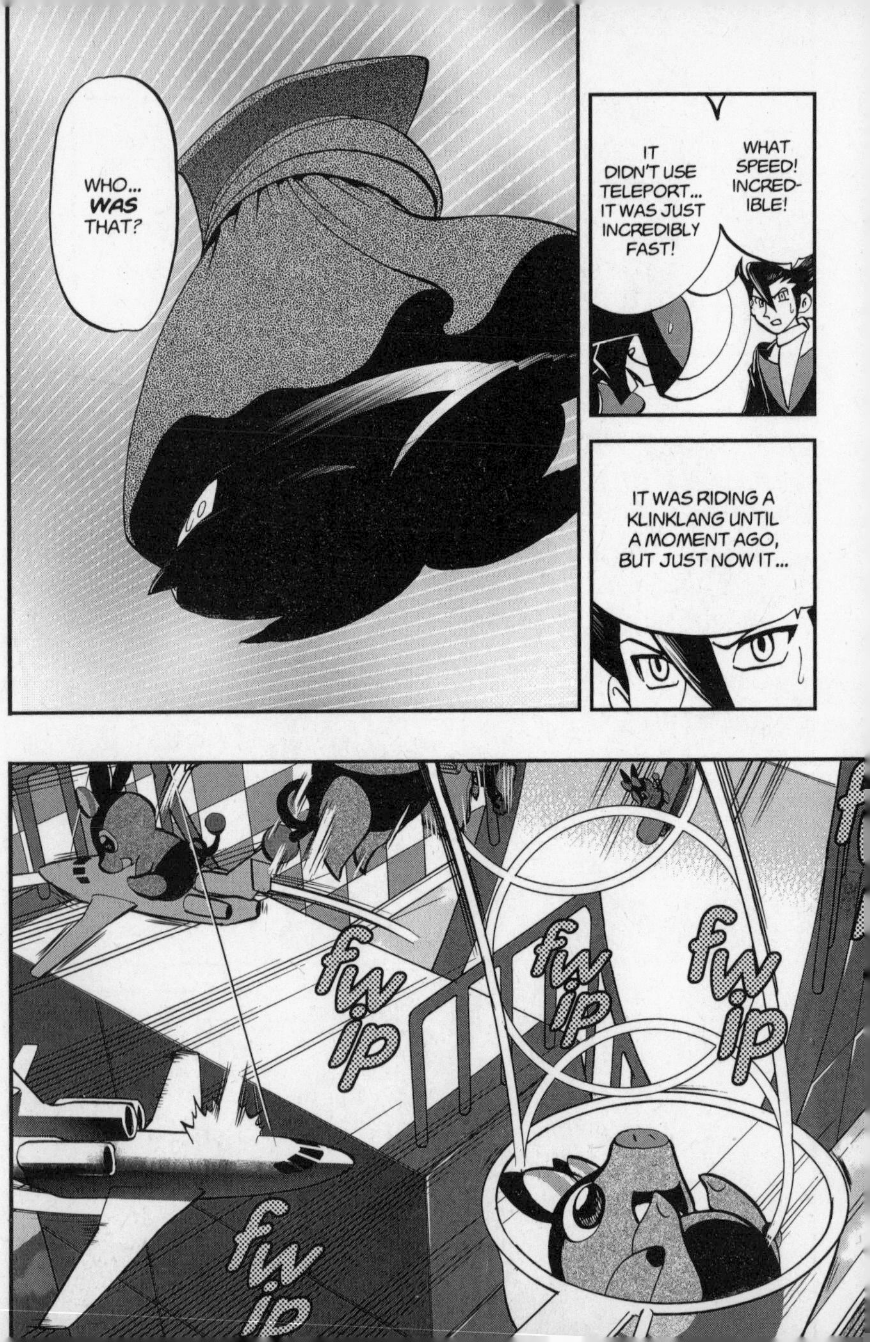
WHAT SPEED! INCRED-IBLE!
IT DIDN'T USE TELEPORT... IT WAS JUST INCREDIBLY FAST!
IT WAS RIDING A KLINKLANG UNTIL A MOMENT AGO, BUT JUST NOW IT...
WHO... **WAS** THAT?
fwip
fwip
fwip

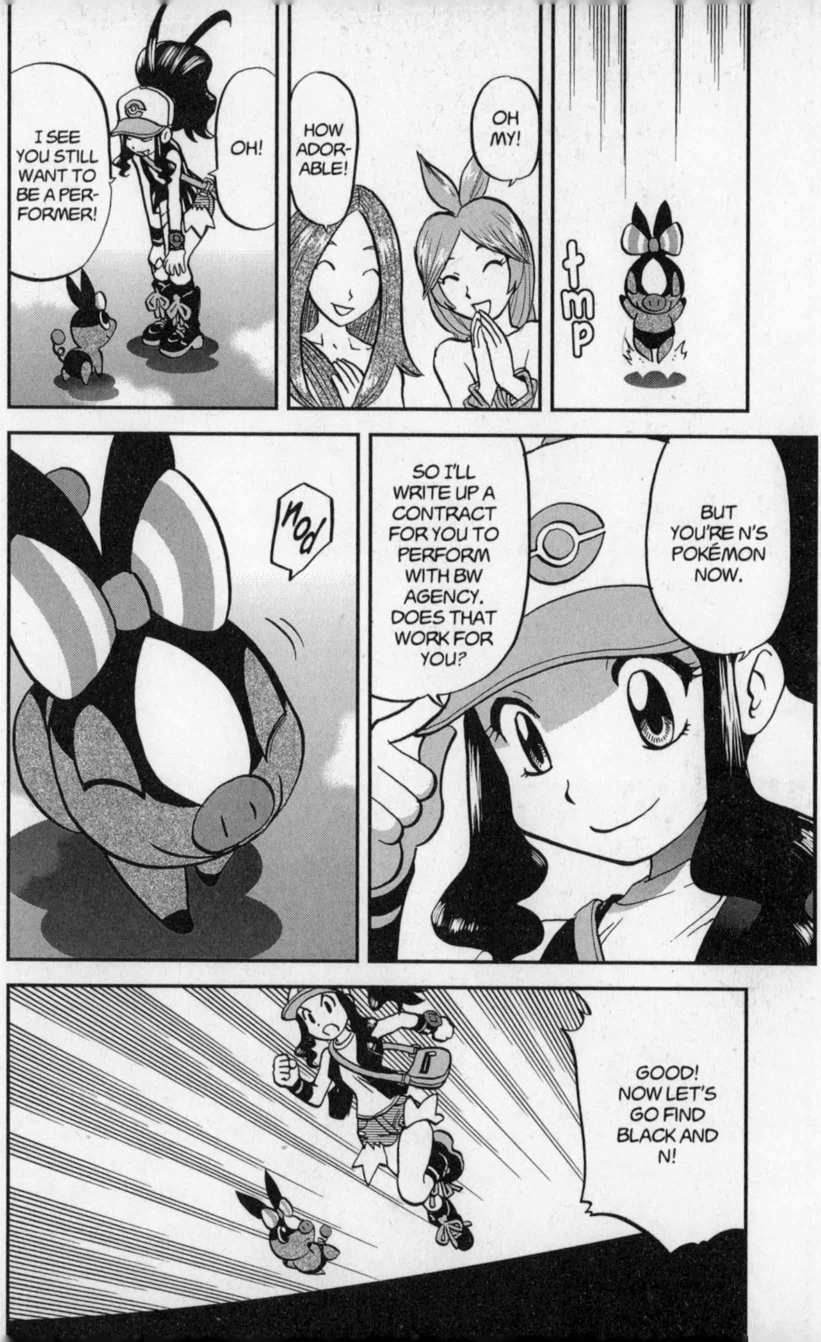
tmp
OH MY!
HOW ADOR-ABLE!
OH!
I SEE YOU STILL WANT TO BE A PER-FORMER!
BUT YOU'RE N'S POKÉMON NOW.
SO I'LL WRITE UP A CONTRACT FOR YOU TO PERFORM WITH BW AGENCY. DOES THAT WORK FOR YOU?
nod
GOOD! NOW LET'S GO FIND BLACK AND N!

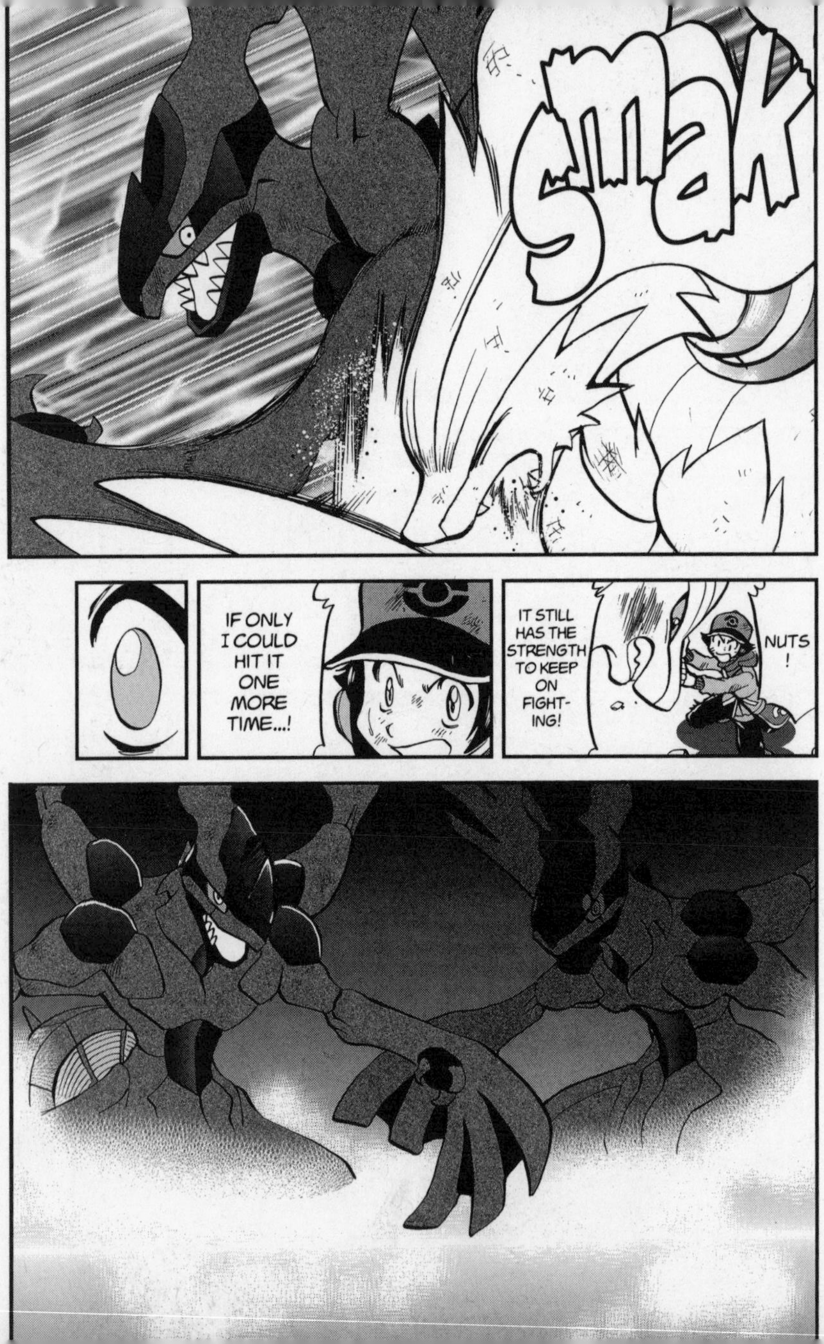
SMAK
NUTS!
IT STILL HAS THE STRENGTH TO KEEP ON FIGHT-ING!
IF ONLY I COULD HIT IT ONE MORE TIME...!

TWO
ZEK-
ROMS
?!

WHAT
THE...?

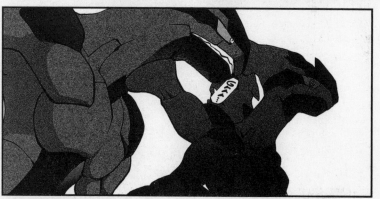

NOW,
RESHIRAM!

foosh

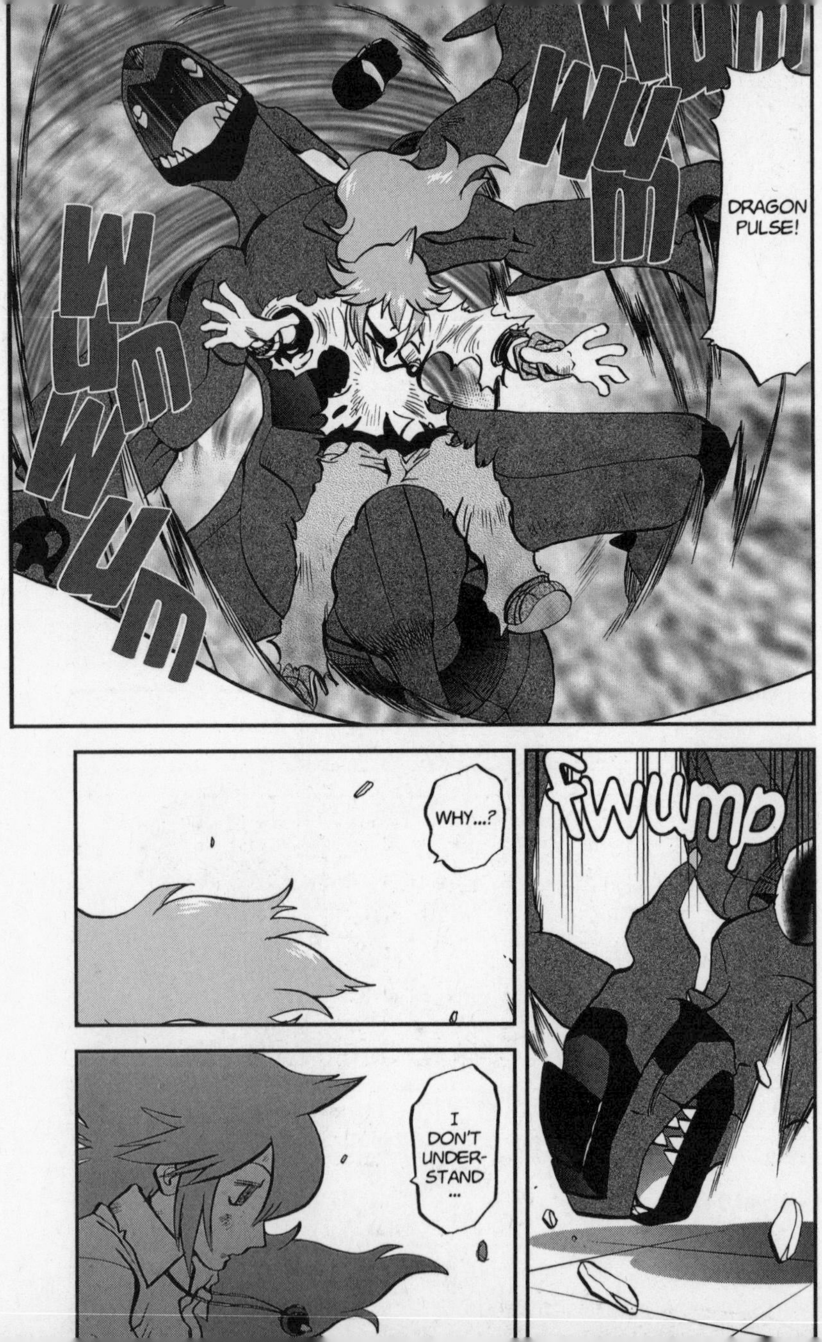
WUM
DRAGON PULSE!
WUM
fwump
WHY...?
I DON'T UNDER-STAND...

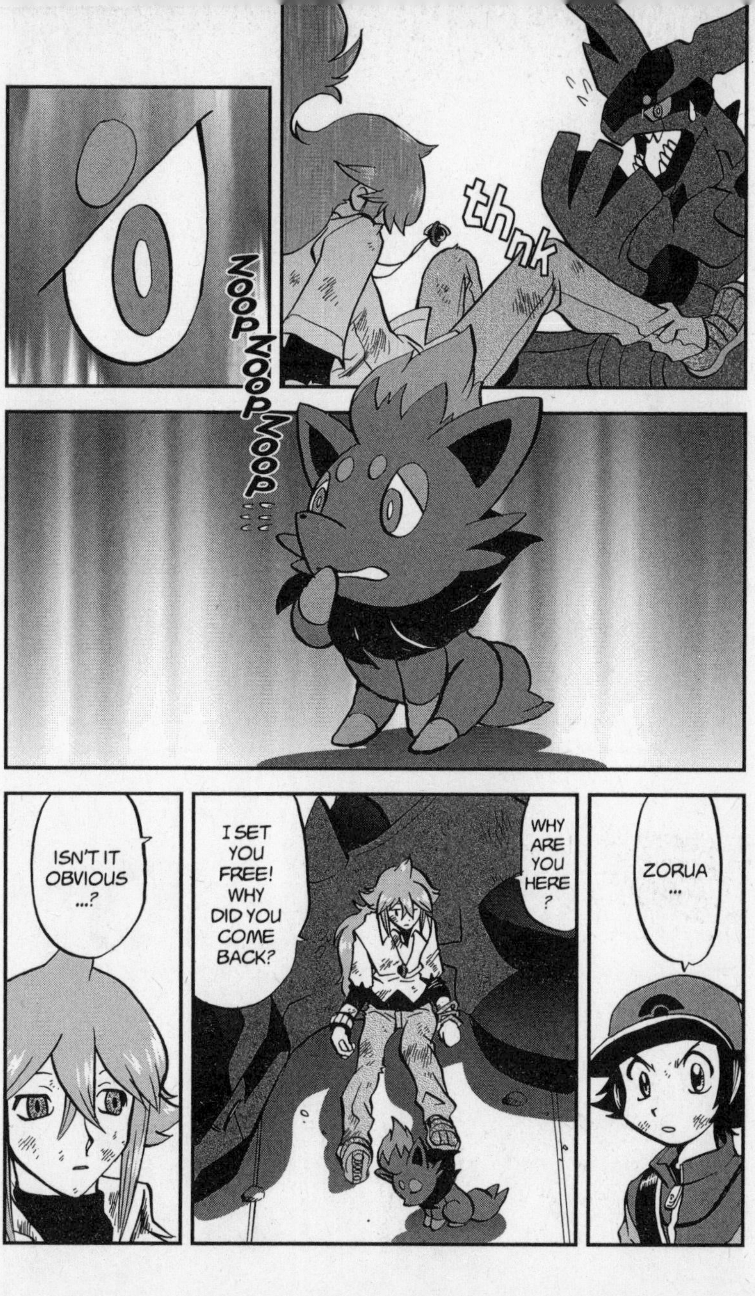
thnk
ZOOP ZOOP ZOOP
ZORUA ...
WHY ARE YOU HERE?
I SET YOU FREE! WHY DID YOU COME BACK?
ISN'T IT OBVIOUS ...?

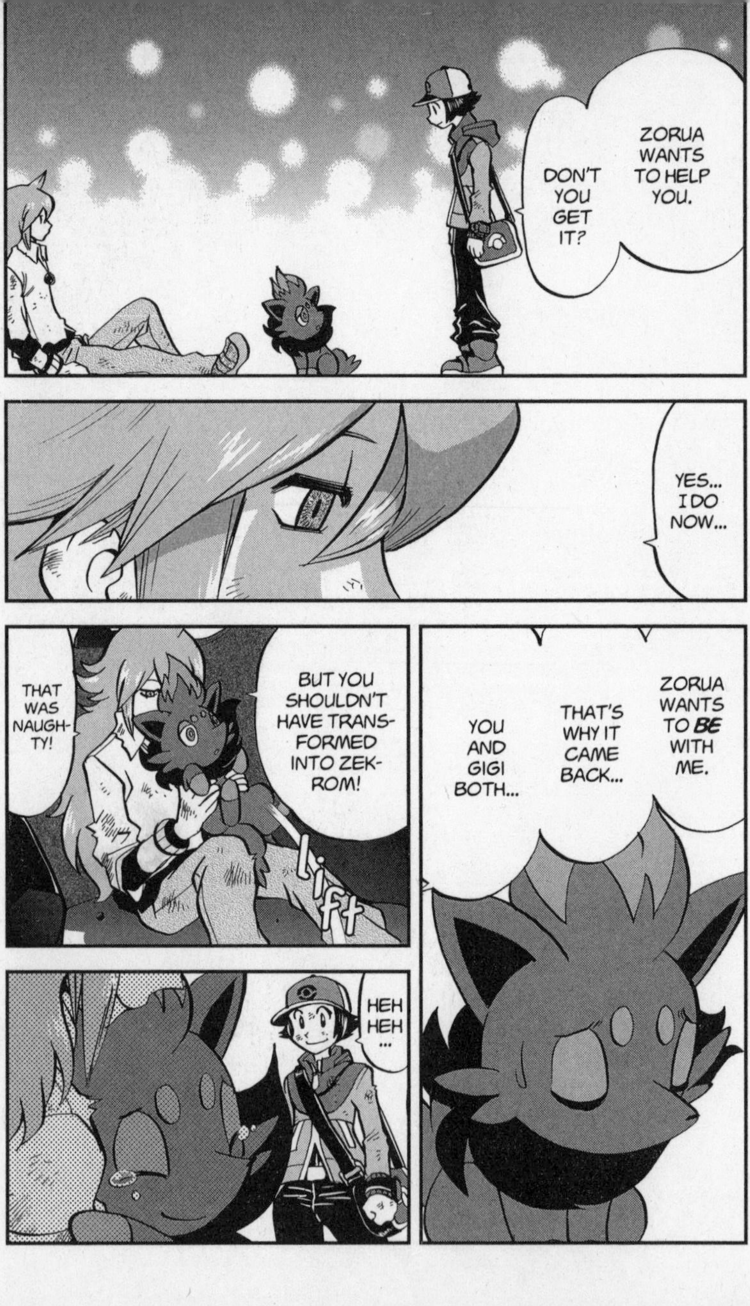
ZORUA WANTS TO HELP YOU.
DON'T YOU GET IT?
YES... I DO NOW...
ZORUA WANTS TO *BE* WITH ME.
THAT'S WHY IT CAME BACK...
YOU AND GIGI BOTH...
BUT YOU SHOULDN'T HAVE TRANSFORMED INTO ZEKROM!
THAT WAS NAUGHTY!
lift
HEH HEH ...

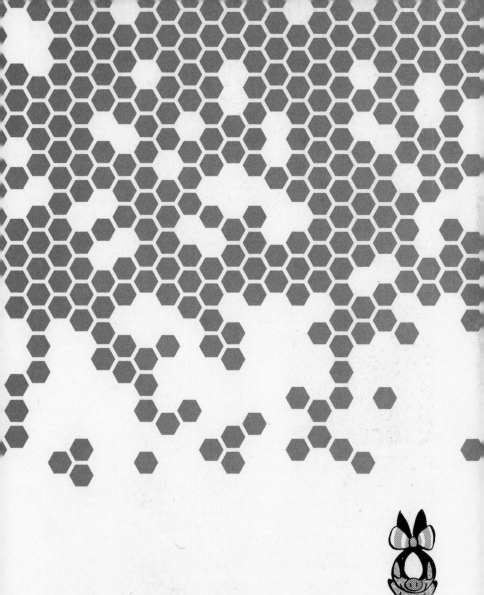

Adventure 66 Truth Revealed

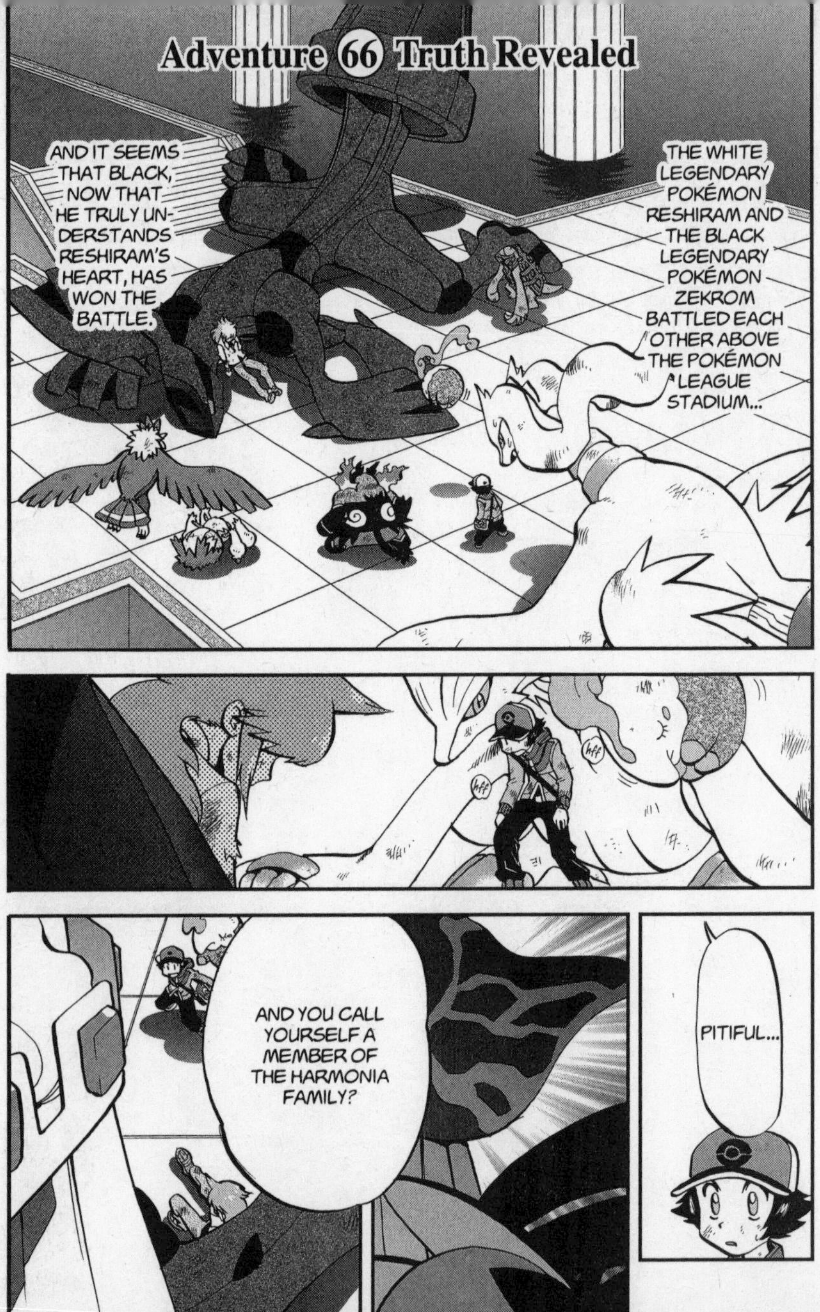
THE WHITE LEGENDARY POKÉMON RESHIRAM AND THE BLACK LEGENDARY POKÉMON ZEKROM BATTLED EACH OTHER ABOVE THE POKÉMON LEAGUE STADIUM...
AND IT SEEMS THAT BLACK, NOW THAT HE TRULY UNDERSTANDS RESHIRAM'S HEART, HAS WON THE BATTLE.
hff
hff
PITIFUL...
AND YOU CALL YOURSELF A MEMBER OF THE HARMONIA FAMILY?

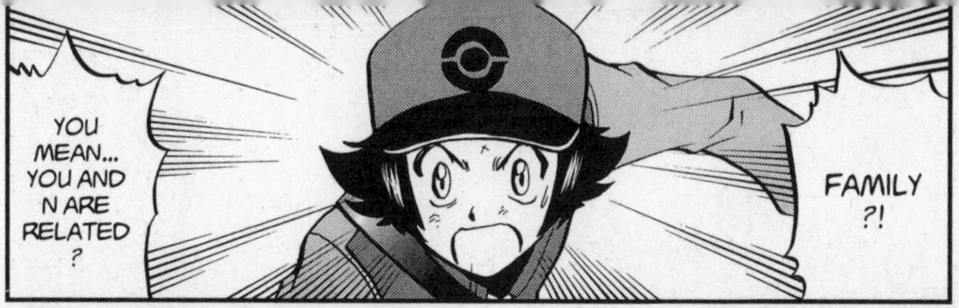
YOU MEAN... YOU AND N ARE RELATED ?
FAMILY ?!
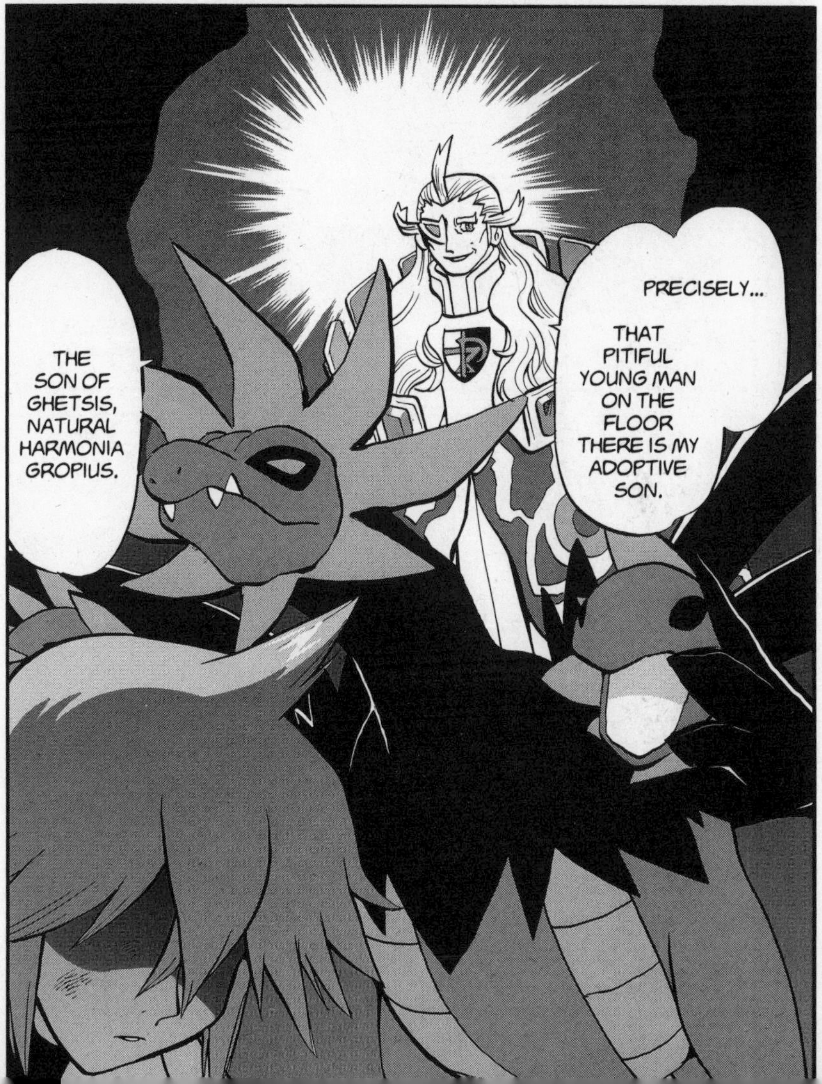
PRECISELY...
THAT PITIFUL YOUNG MAN ON THE FLOOR THERE IS MY ADOPTIVE SON.
THE SON OF GHETSIS, NATURAL HARMONIA GROPIUS.

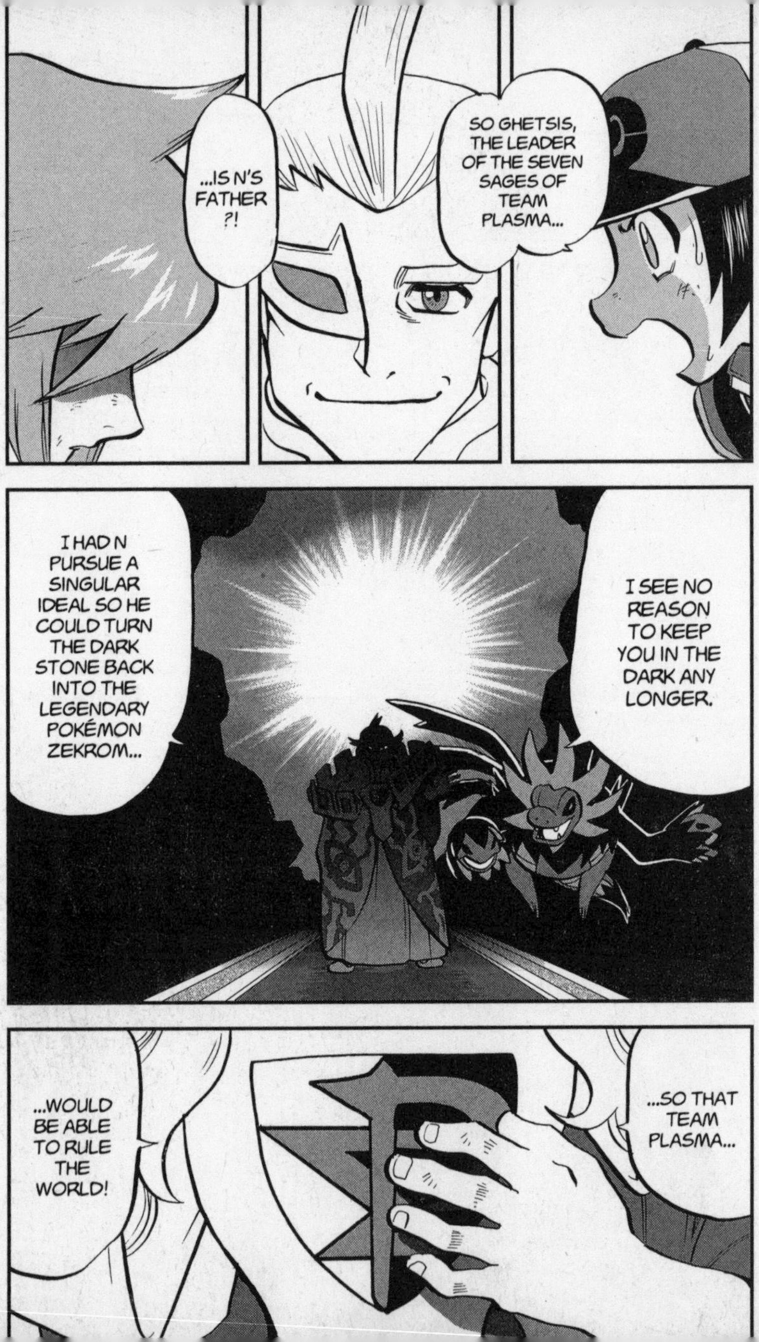
SO GHETSIS, THE LEADER OF THE SEVEN SAGES OF TEAM PLASMA...
...IS N'S FATHER ?!
I SEE NO REASON TO KEEP YOU IN THE DARK ANY LONGER.
I HAD N PURSUE A SINGULAR IDEAL SO HE COULD TURN THE DARK STONE BACK INTO THE LEGENDARY POKÉMON ZEKROM...
...SO THAT TEAM PLASMA...
...WOULD BE ABLE TO RULE THE WORLD!

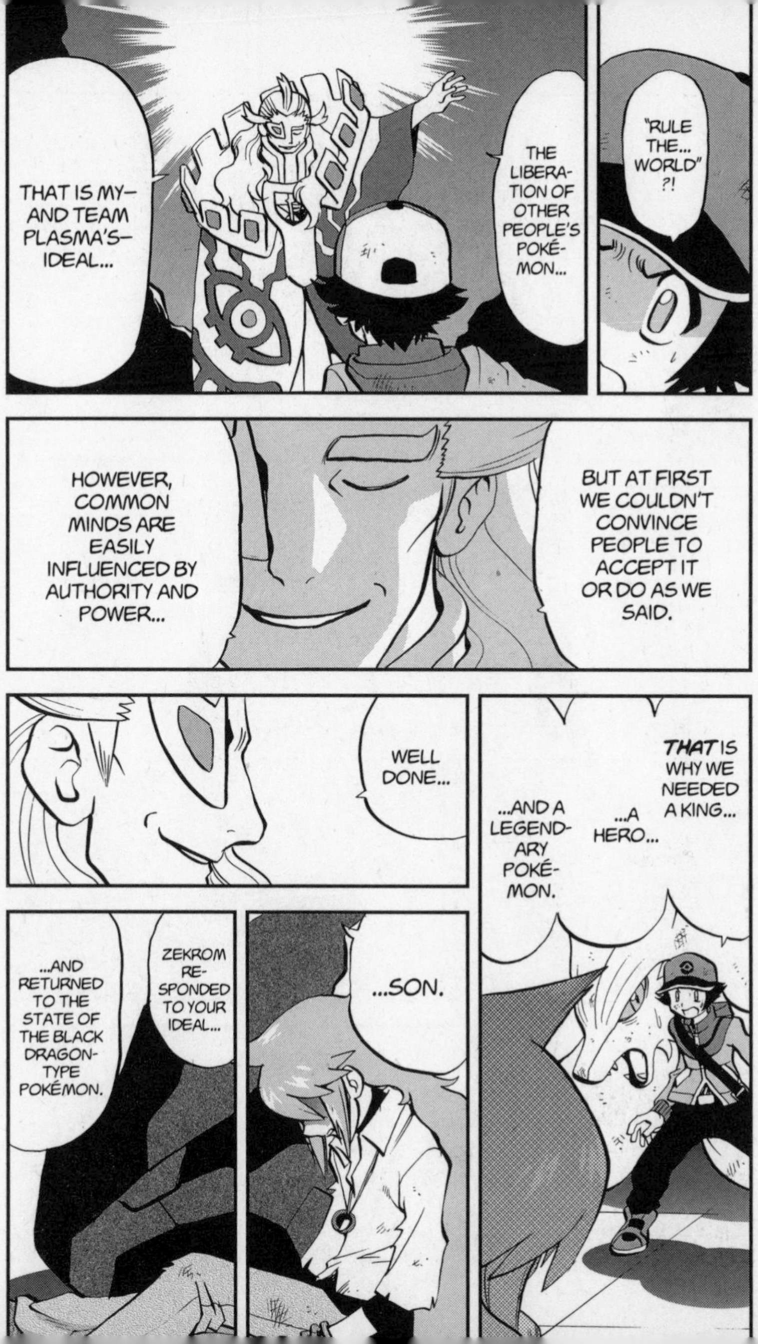
"RULE THE... WORLD"?!
THE LIBERATION OF OTHER PEOPLE'S POKÉMON...
THAT IS MY— AND TEAM PLASMA'S— IDEAL...
BUT AT FIRST WE COULDN'T CONVINCE PEOPLE TO ACCEPT IT OR DO AS WE SAID.
HOWEVER, COMMON MINDS ARE EASILY INFLUENCED BY AUTHORITY AND POWER...
THAT IS WHY WE NEEDED A KING...
...A HERO...
...AND A LEGENDARY POKÉMON.
WELL DONE...
...SON.
ZEKROM RESPONDED TO YOUR IDEAL...
...AND RETURNED TO THE STATE OF THE BLACK DRAGON-TYPE POKÉMON.

THE CHAMPION, ALDER, WAS DEFEATED. THE GYM LEADERS WERE CAPTURED. WE TOOK OVER THE POKÉMON LEAGUE STADIUM.
AND ALL OF UNOVA WITNESSED THEIR POWERLESSNESS IN COMPARISON TO TEAM PLASMA.
CONSEQUENTLY, THEY DECIDED THERE MUST BE SOMETHING TO OUR MESSAGE! BECAUSE IGNORANT PEOPLE THINK "MIGHT IS RIGHT." AND NOW THEY ARE READY AND WILLING TO BEND TO OUR AUTHORITY AND FOLLOW OUR EVERY COMMAND!
WE KNEW WE COULD MANIPULATE PEOPLE INTO FOLLOWING TEAM PLASMA AND ACCEPTING OUR SUPPOSED IDEAL.
YES...
EVERYTHING WAS GOING ACCORDING TO PLAN...
... UNTIL ...
...MY FOOL OF A SON...
...DECIDED TO BATTLE THE HERO OF TRUTH AND RESHIRAM.
IT WAS AS IF HE WANTED TO PROVE HE WAS REALLY A HERO!

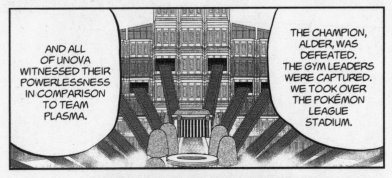

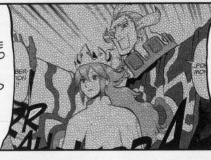

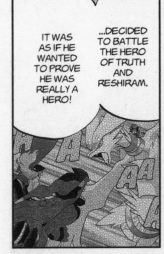

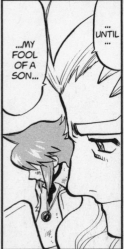

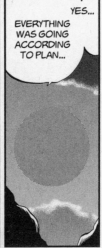

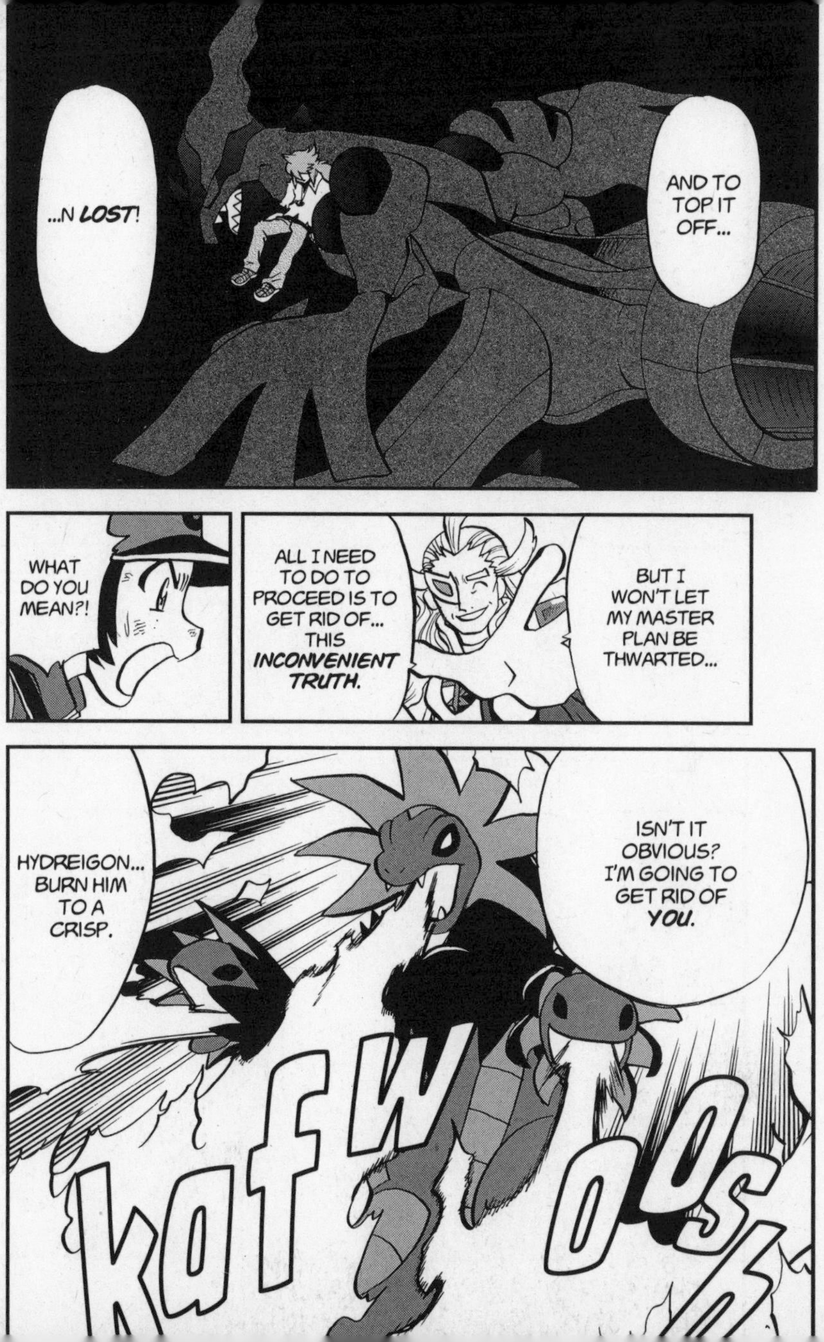
AND TO TOP IT OFF...
...N LOST!
BUT I WON'T LET MY MASTER PLAN BE THWARTED...
ALL I NEED TO DO TO PROCEED IS TO GET RID OF... THIS INCONVENIENT TRUTH.
WHAT DO YOU MEAN?!
ISN'T IT OBVIOUS? I'M GOING TO GET RID OF YOU.
HYDREIGON... BURN HIM TO A CRISP.
KAFWOOSH

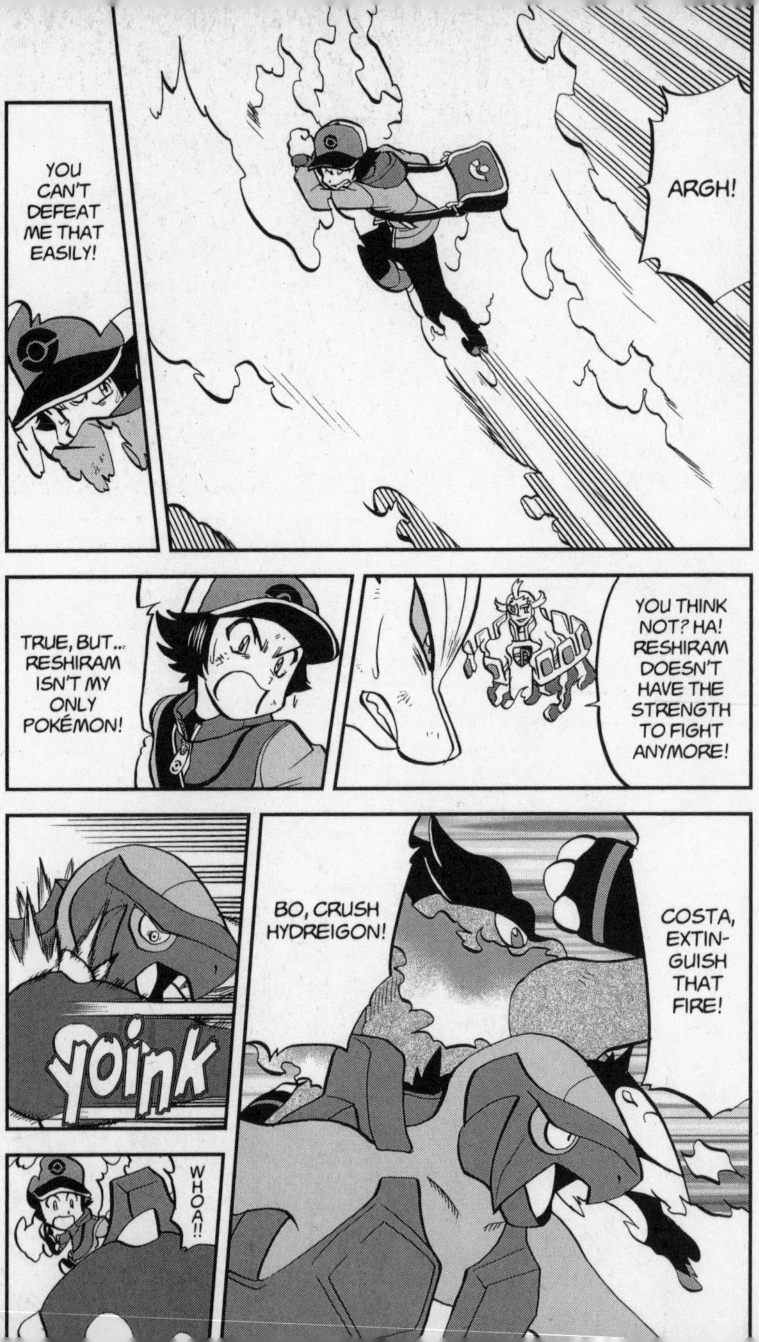
ARGH!
YOU CAN'T DEFEAT ME THAT EASILY!
YOU THINK NOT? HA! RESHIRAM DOESN'T HAVE THE STRENGTH TO FIGHT ANYMORE!
TRUE, BUT... RESHIRAM ISN'T MY ONLY POKÉMON!
COSTA, EXTIN-GUISH THAT FIRE!
BO, CRUSH HYDREIGON!
yoink
WHOA!!

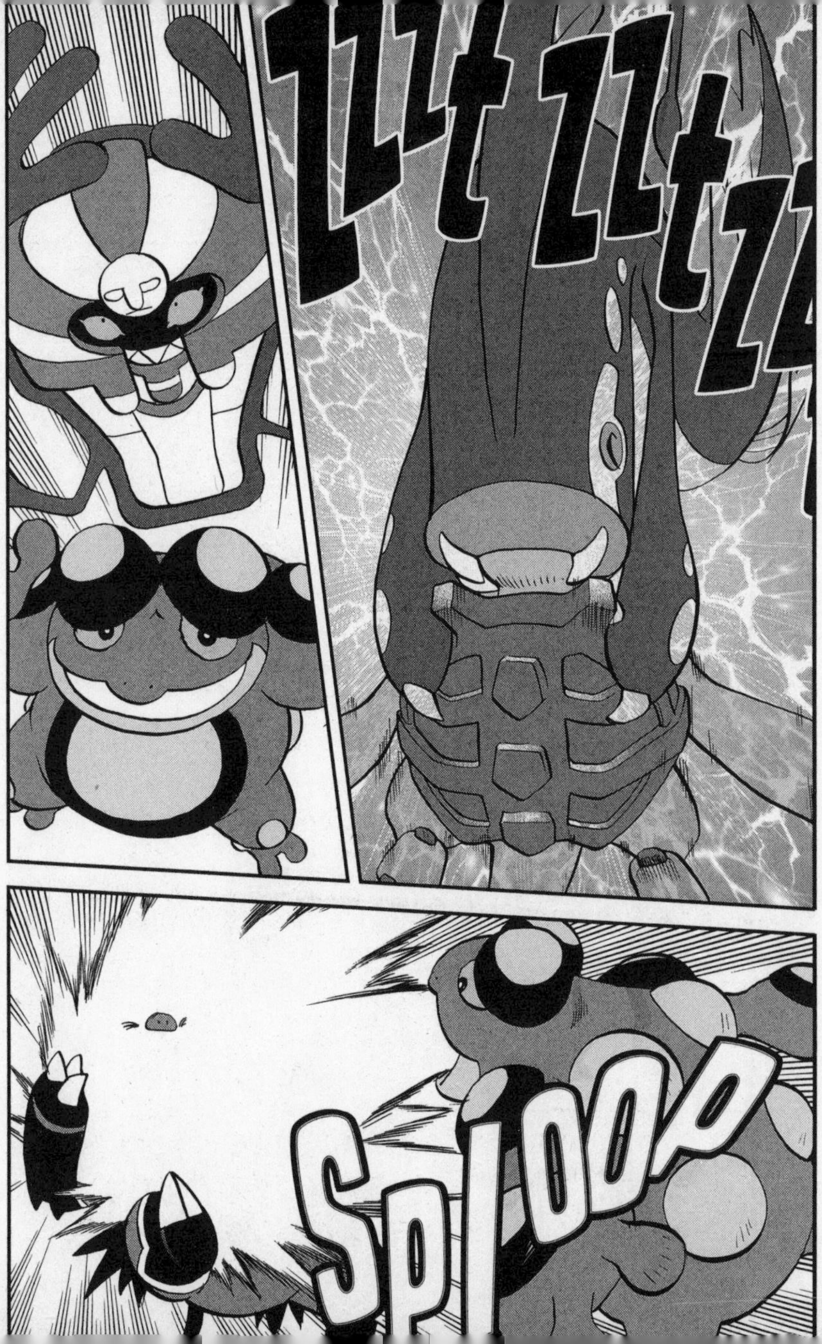
ZZZT ZZZT ZZ
SPLOOP

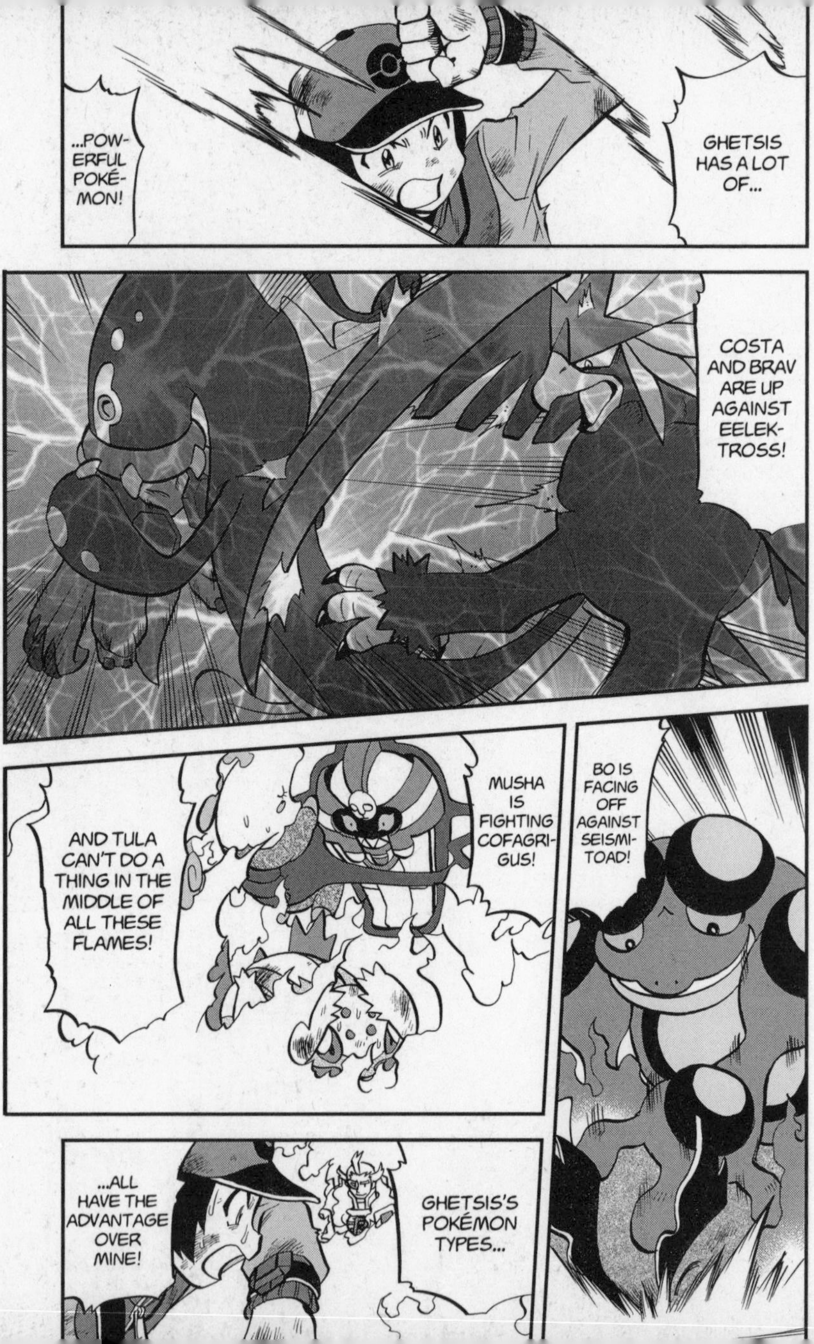
GHETSIS HAS A LOT OF...
...POWERFUL POKÉMON!
COSTA AND BRAV ARE UP AGAINST EELEKTROSS!
BO IS FACING OFF AGAINST SEISMITOAD!
MUSHA IS FIGHTING COFAGRIGUS!
AND TULA CAN'T DO A THING IN THE MIDDLE OF ALL THESE FLAMES!
GHETSIS'S POKÉMON TYPES...
...ALL HAVE THE ADVANTAGE OVER MINE!

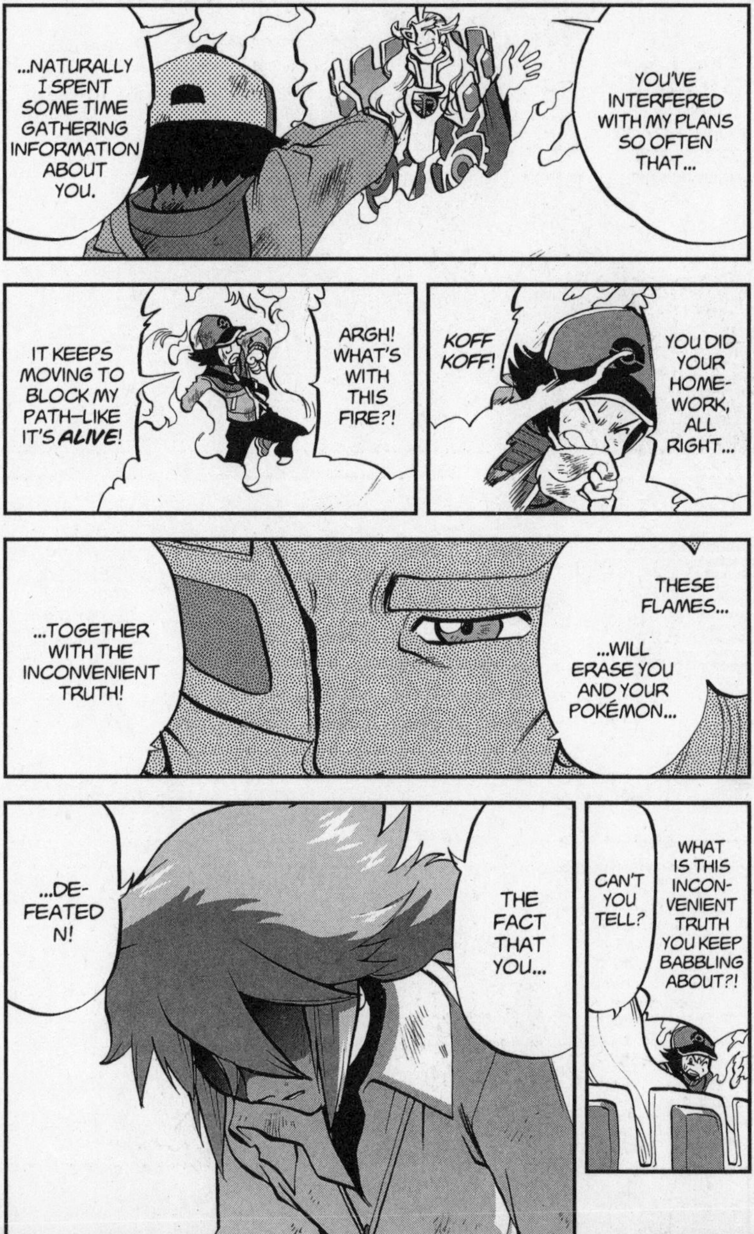
YOU'VE INTERFERED WITH MY PLANS SO OFTEN THAT...
...NATURALLY I SPENT SOME TIME GATHERING INFORMATION ABOUT YOU.
YOU DID YOUR HOME-WORK, ALL RIGHT...
KOFF KOFF!
ARGH! WHAT'S WITH THIS FIRE?!
IT KEEPS MOVING TO BLOCK MY PATH—LIKE IT'S *ALIVE*!
THESE FLAMES...
...WILL ERASE YOU AND YOUR POKÉMON...
...TOGETHER WITH THE INCONVENIENT TRUTH!
WHAT IS THIS INCON-VENIENT TRUTH YOU KEEP BABBLING ABOUT?!
CAN'T YOU TELL?
THE FACT THAT YOU...
...DE-FEATED N!

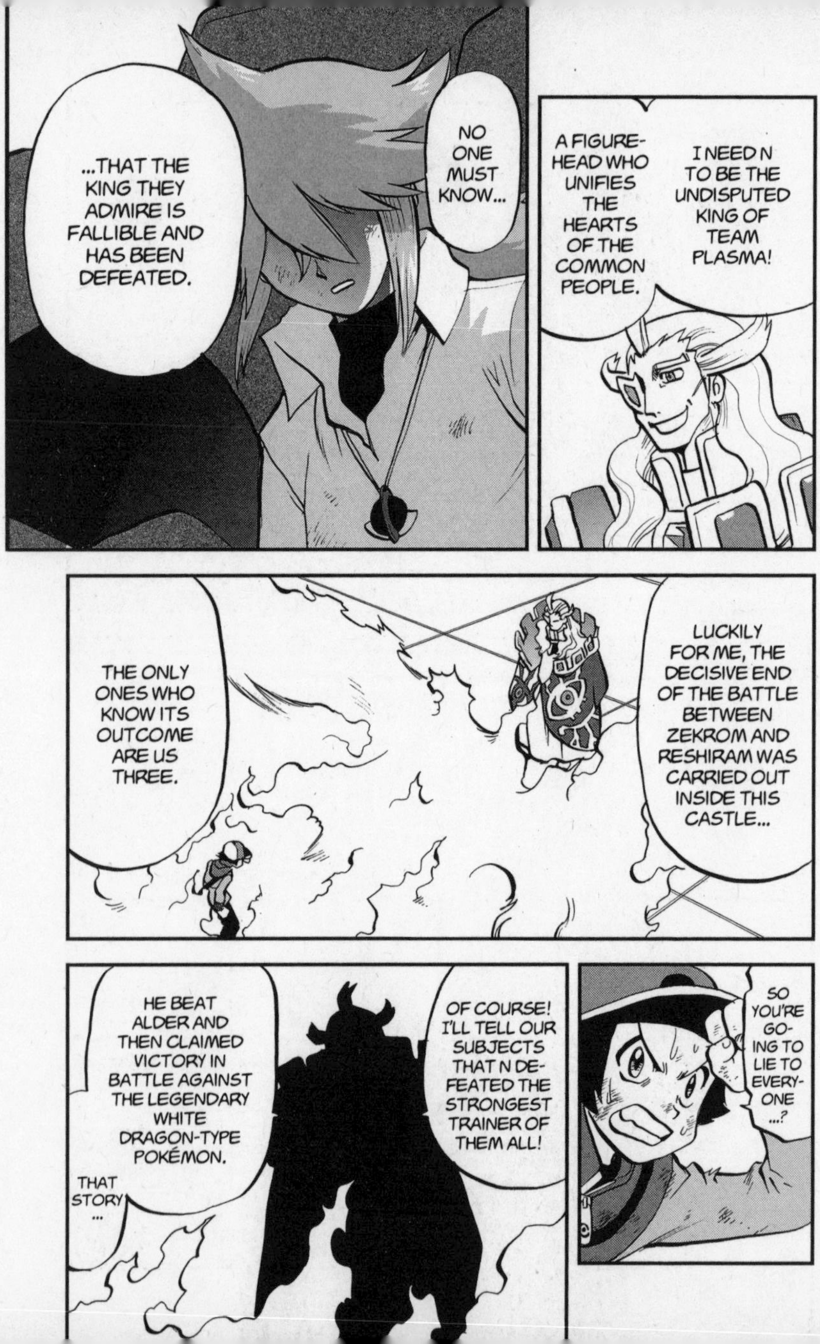
I NEED N TO BE THE UNDISPUTED KING OF TEAM PLASMA!
A FIGURE-HEAD WHO UNIFIES THE HEARTS OF THE COMMON PEOPLE.
NO ONE MUST KNOW...
...THAT THE KING THEY ADMIRE IS FALLIBLE AND HAS BEEN DEFEATED.
LUCKILY FOR ME, THE DECISIVE END OF THE BATTLE BETWEEN ZEKROM AND RESHIRAM WAS CARRIED OUT INSIDE THIS CASTLE...
THE ONLY ONES WHO KNOW ITS OUTCOME ARE US THREE.
SO YOU'RE GOING TO LIE TO EVERYONE ...?
OF COURSE! I'LL TELL OUR SUBJECTS THAT N DEFEATED THE STRONGEST TRAINER OF THEM ALL!
HE BEAT ALDER AND THEN CLAIMED VICTORY IN BATTLE AGAINST THE LEGENDARY WHITE DRAGON-TYPE POKÉMON.
THAT STORY ...

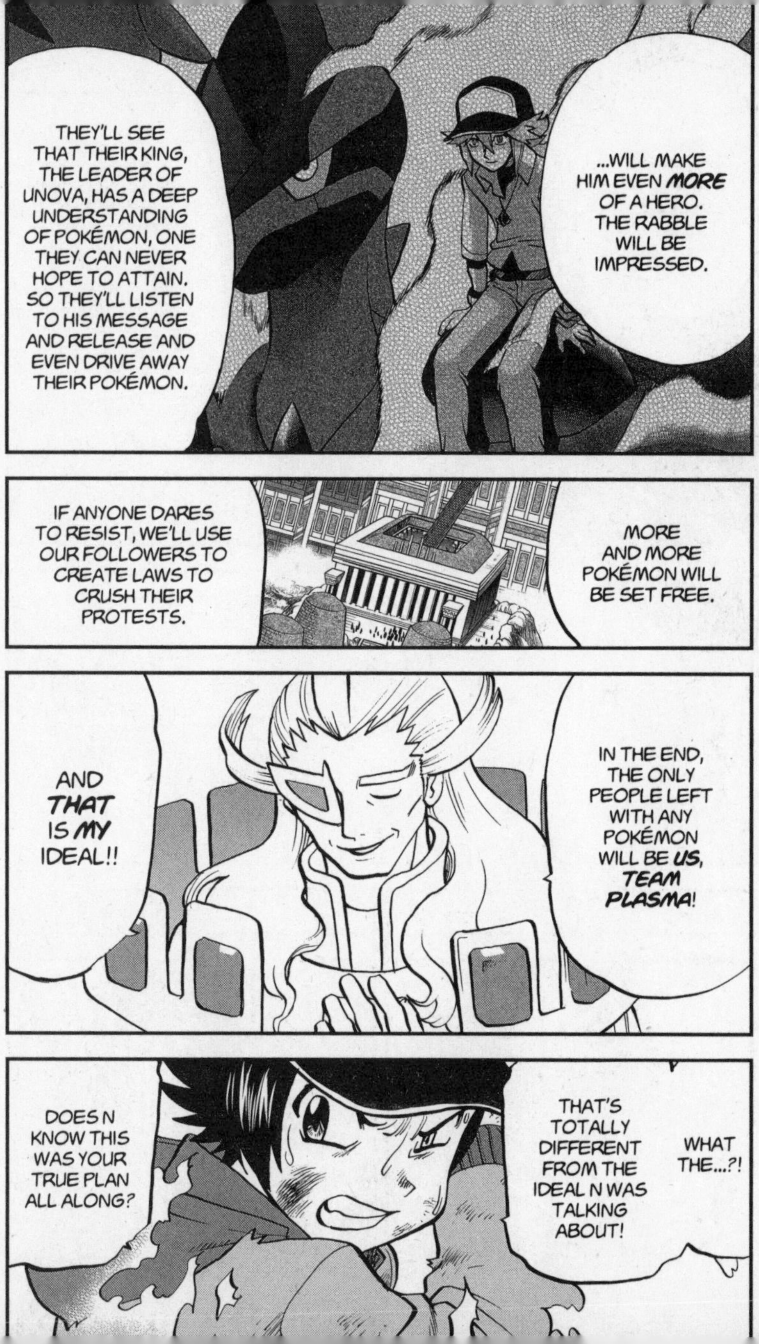
...WILL MAKE HIM EVEN MORE OF A HERO. THE RABBLE WILL BE IMPRESSED.
THEY'LL SEE THAT THEIR KING, THE LEADER OF UNOVA, HAS A DEEP UNDERSTANDING OF POKÉMON, ONE THEY CAN NEVER HOPE TO ATTAIN. SO THEY'LL LISTEN TO HIS MESSAGE AND RELEASE AND EVEN DRIVE AWAY THEIR POKÉMON.
MORE AND MORE POKÉMON WILL BE SET FREE.
IF ANYONE DARES TO RESIST, WE'LL USE OUR FOLLOWERS TO CREATE LAWS TO CRUSH THEIR PROTESTS.
IN THE END, THE ONLY PEOPLE LEFT WITH ANY POKÉMON WILL BE US, TEAM PLASMA!
AND THAT IS MY IDEAL!!
WHAT THE...?!
THAT'S TOTALLY DIFFERENT FROM THE IDEAL N WAS TALKING ABOUT!
DOES N KNOW THIS WAS YOUR TRUE PLAN ALL ALONG?

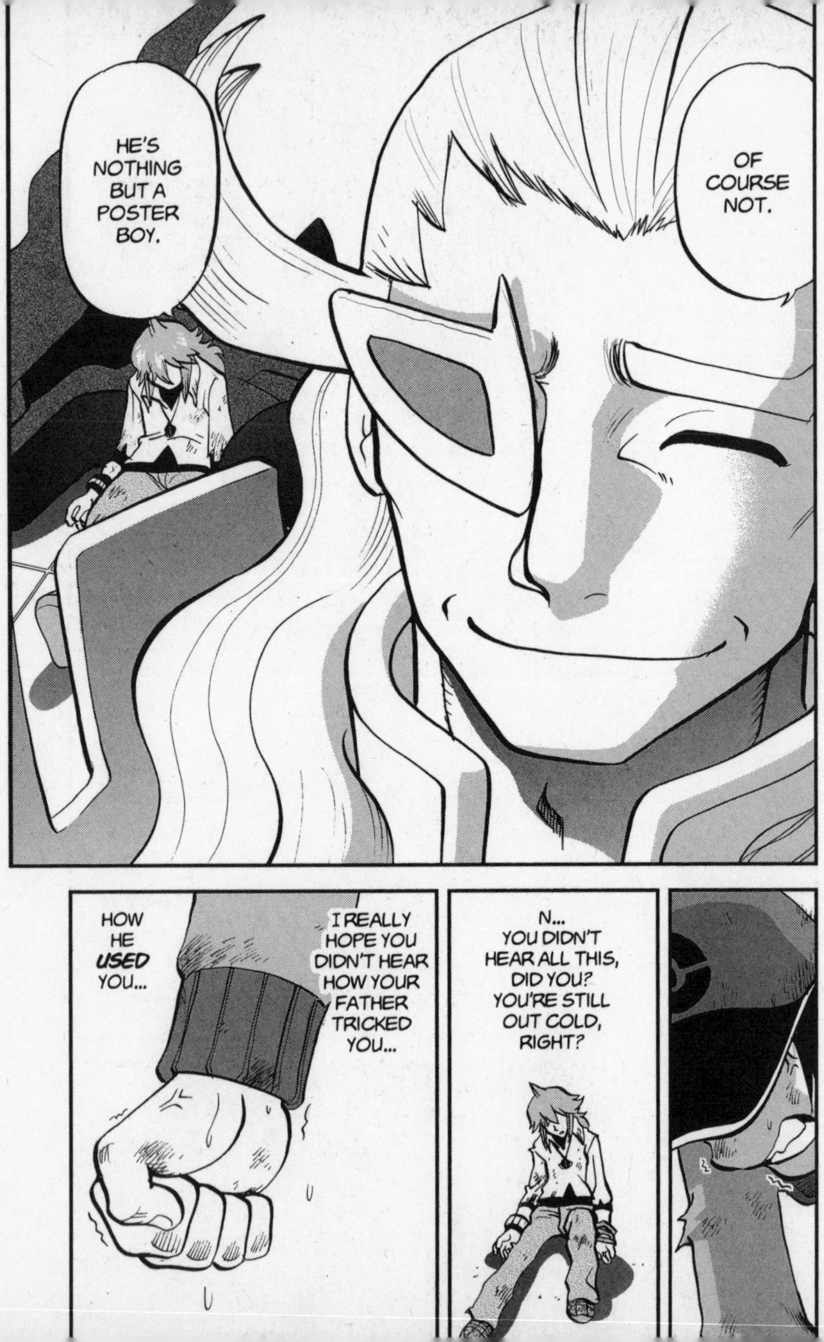
OF COURSE NOT.
HE'S NOTHING BUT A POSTER BOY.
N... YOU DIDN'T HEAR ALL THIS, DID YOU? YOU'RE STILL OUT COLD, RIGHT?
I REALLY HOPE YOU DIDN'T HEAR HOW YOUR FATHER TRICKED YOU...
HOW HE *USED* YOU...

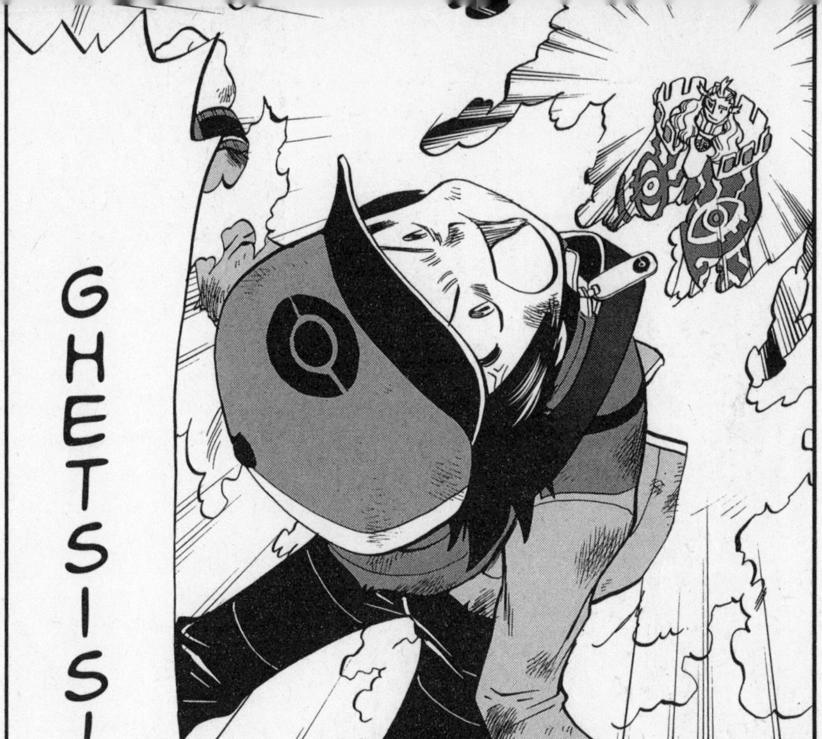
GHETSIS!

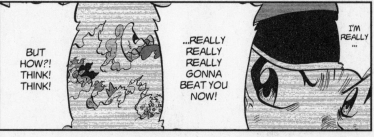

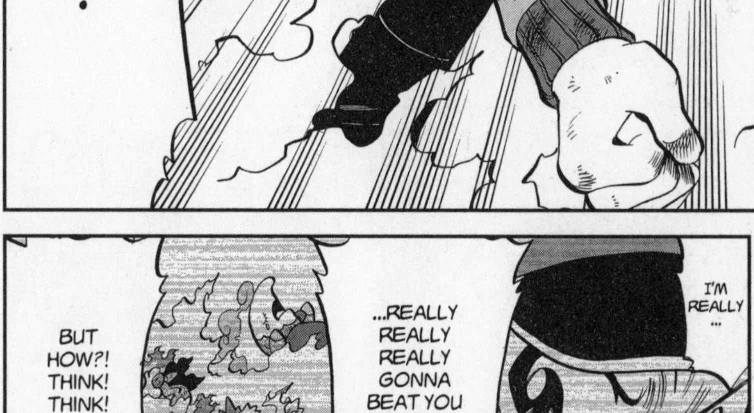
I'M REALLY...
...REALLY REALLY REALLY GONNA BEAT YOU NOW!
BUT HOW?! THINK! THINK!

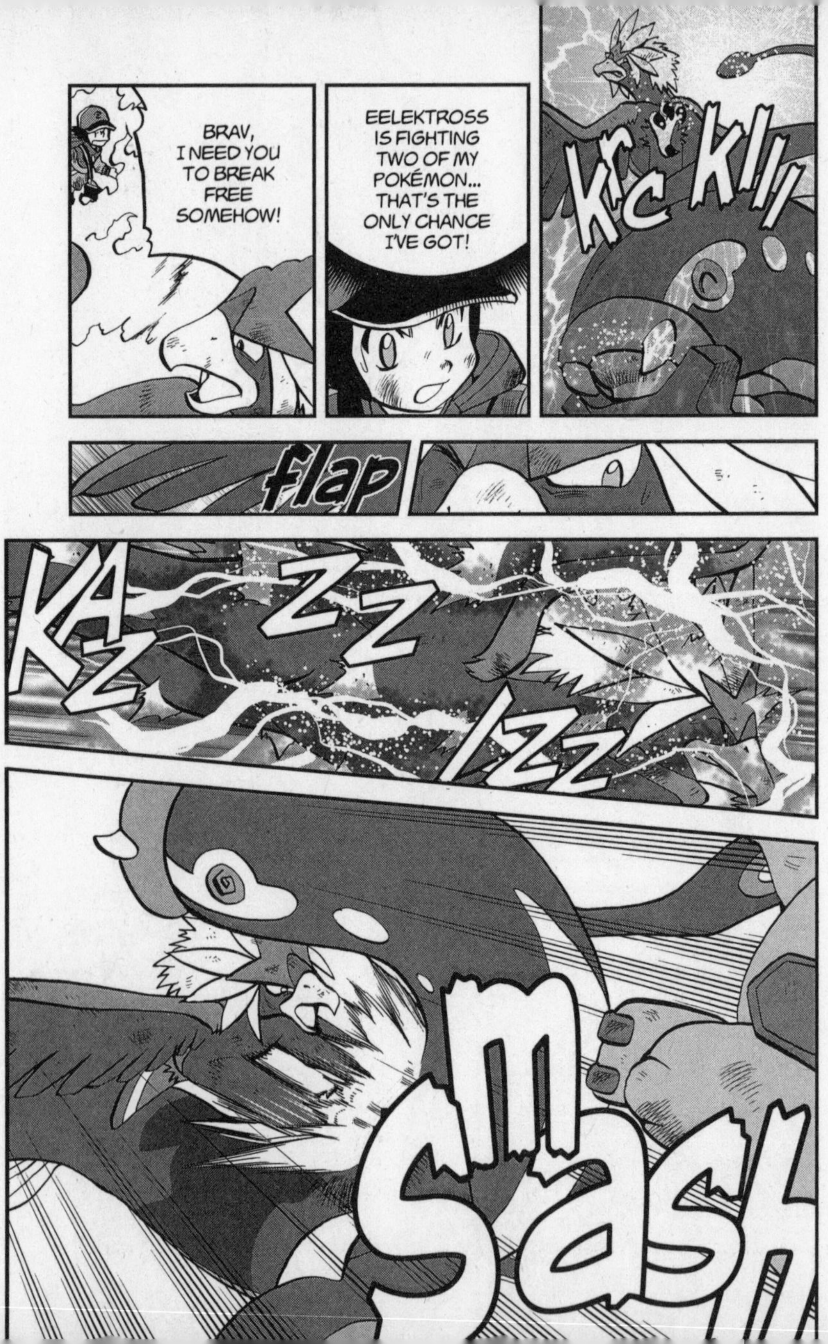
Krc Klll
EELEKTROSS IS FIGHTING TWO OF MY POKÉMON... THAT'S THE ONLY CHANCE I'VE GOT!
BRAV, I NEED YOU TO BREAK FREE SOMEHOW!
flap
KAZZZZZZZ
Smash

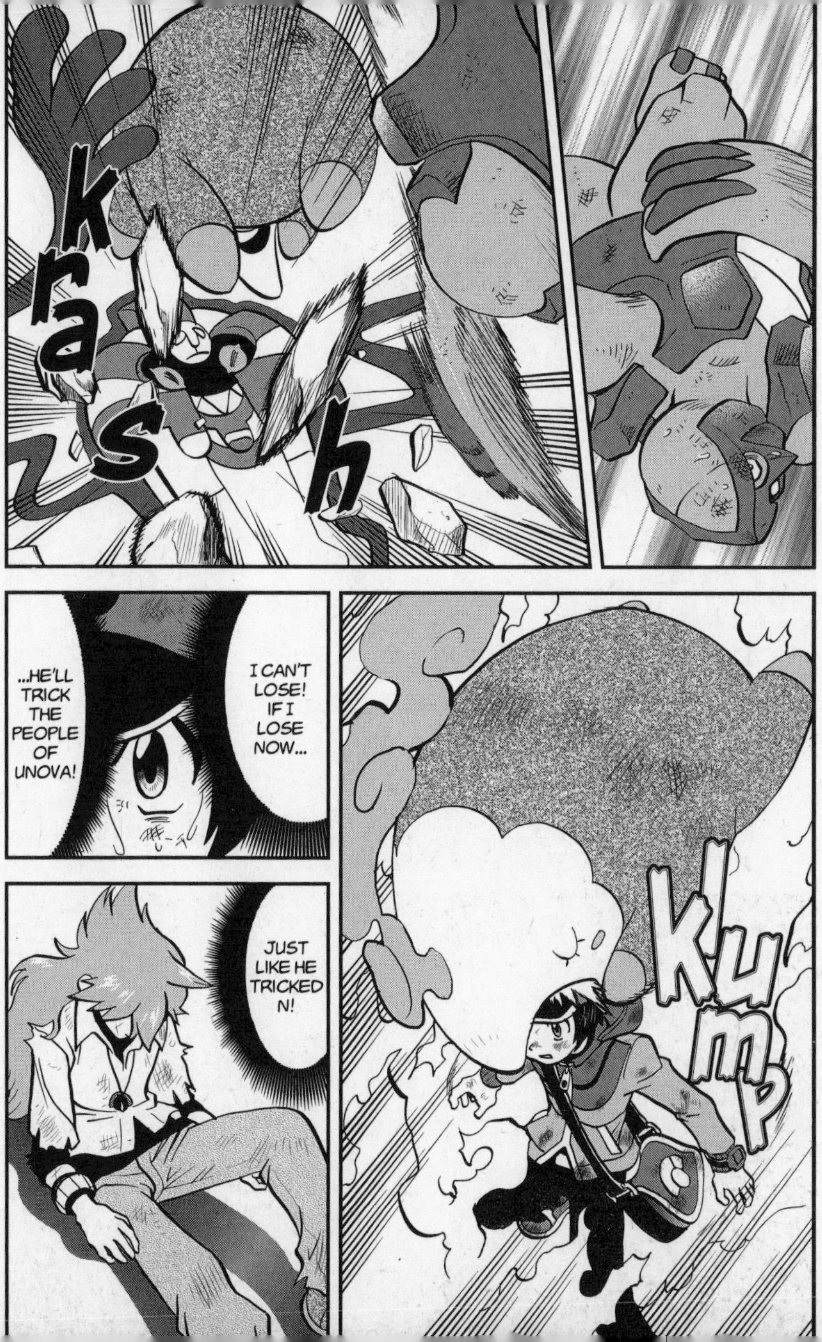
KRASH
KLUMP
I CAN'T LOSE! IF I LOSE NOW...
...HE'LL TRICK THE PEOPLE OF UNOVA!
JUST LIKE HE TRICKED N!

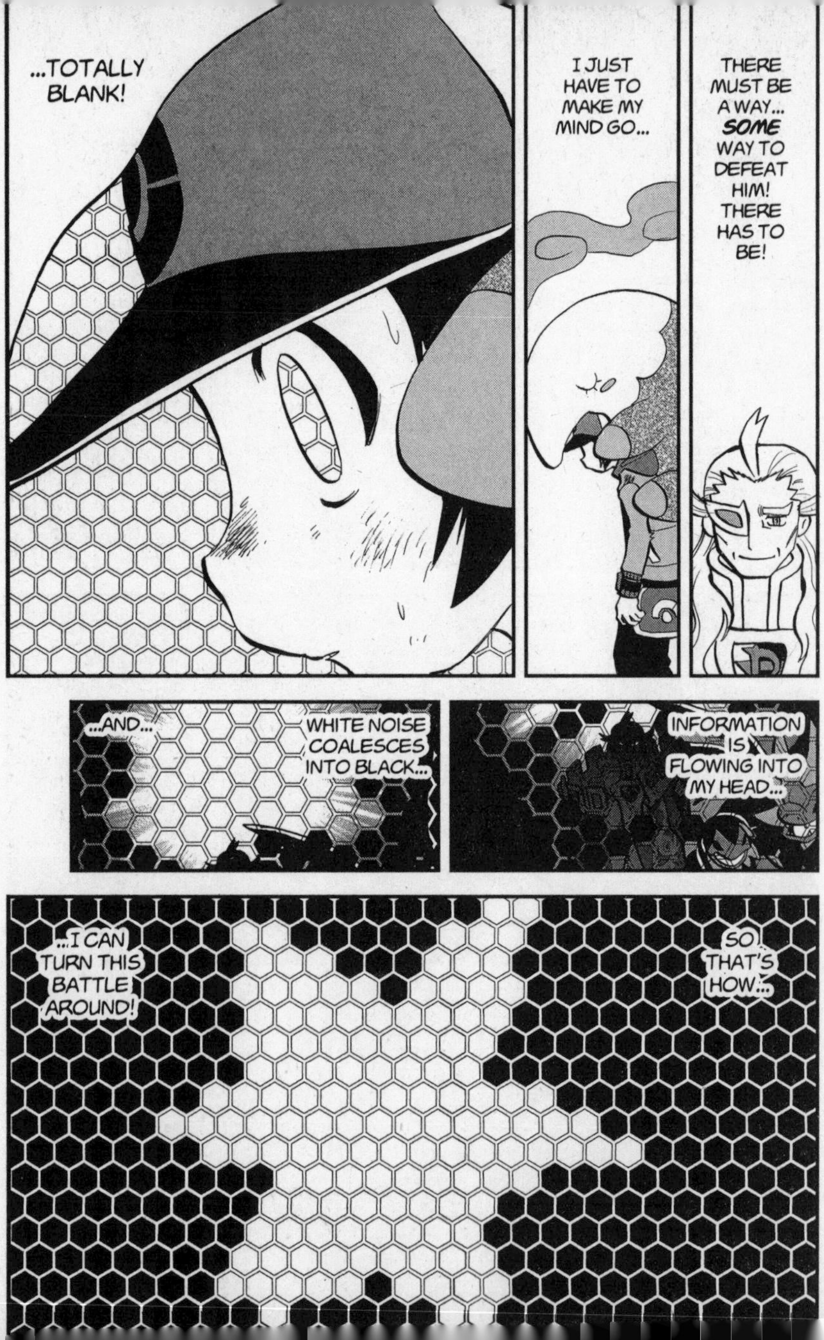
THERE MUST BE A WAY... SOME WAY TO DEFEAT HIM! THERE HAS TO BE!
I JUST HAVE TO MAKE MY MIND GO...
...TOTALLY BLANK!
INFORMATION IS FLOWING INTO MY HEAD...
WHITE NOISE COALESCES INTO BLACK...
...AND...
SO THAT'S HOW...
...I CAN TURN THIS BATTLE AROUND!

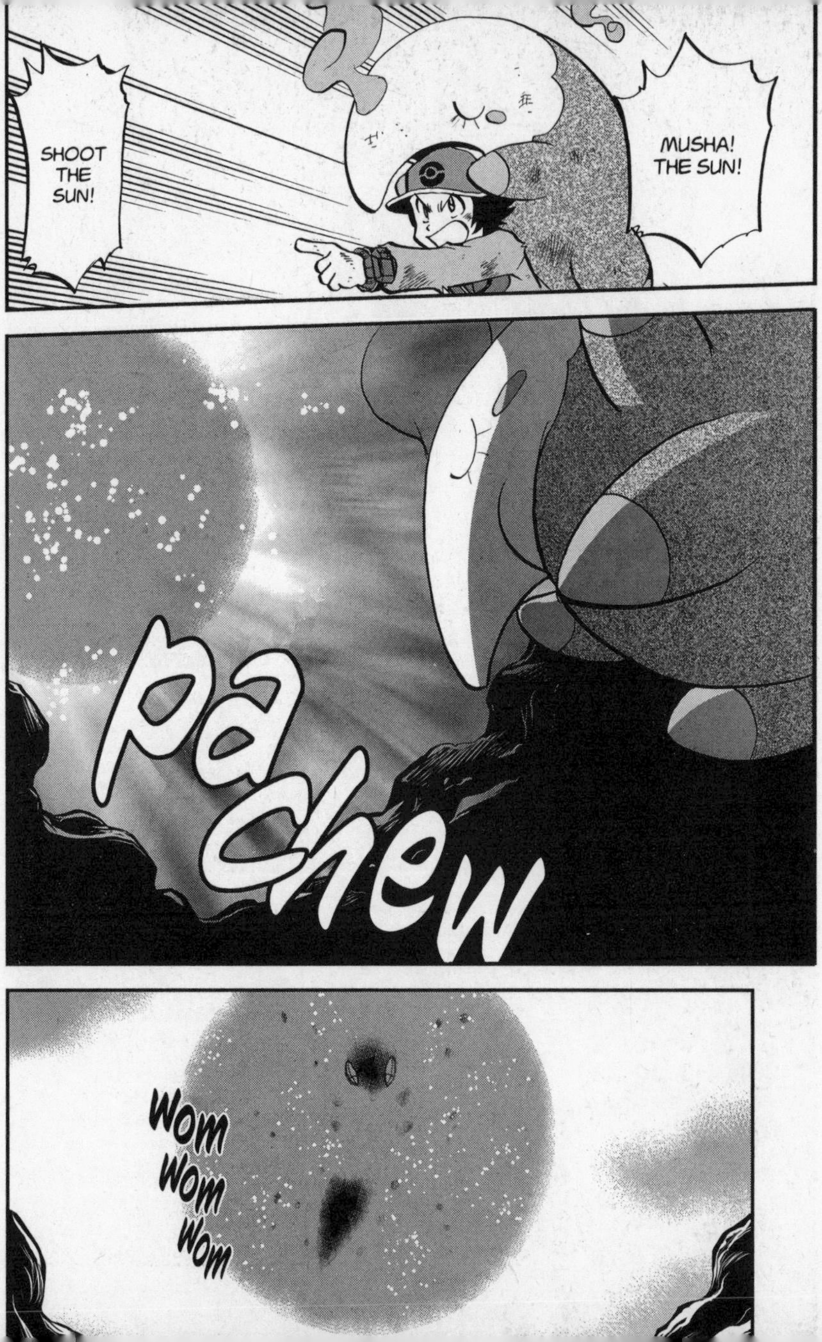
MUSHA! THE SUN!
SHOOT THE SUN!
pachew
wom wom wom wom

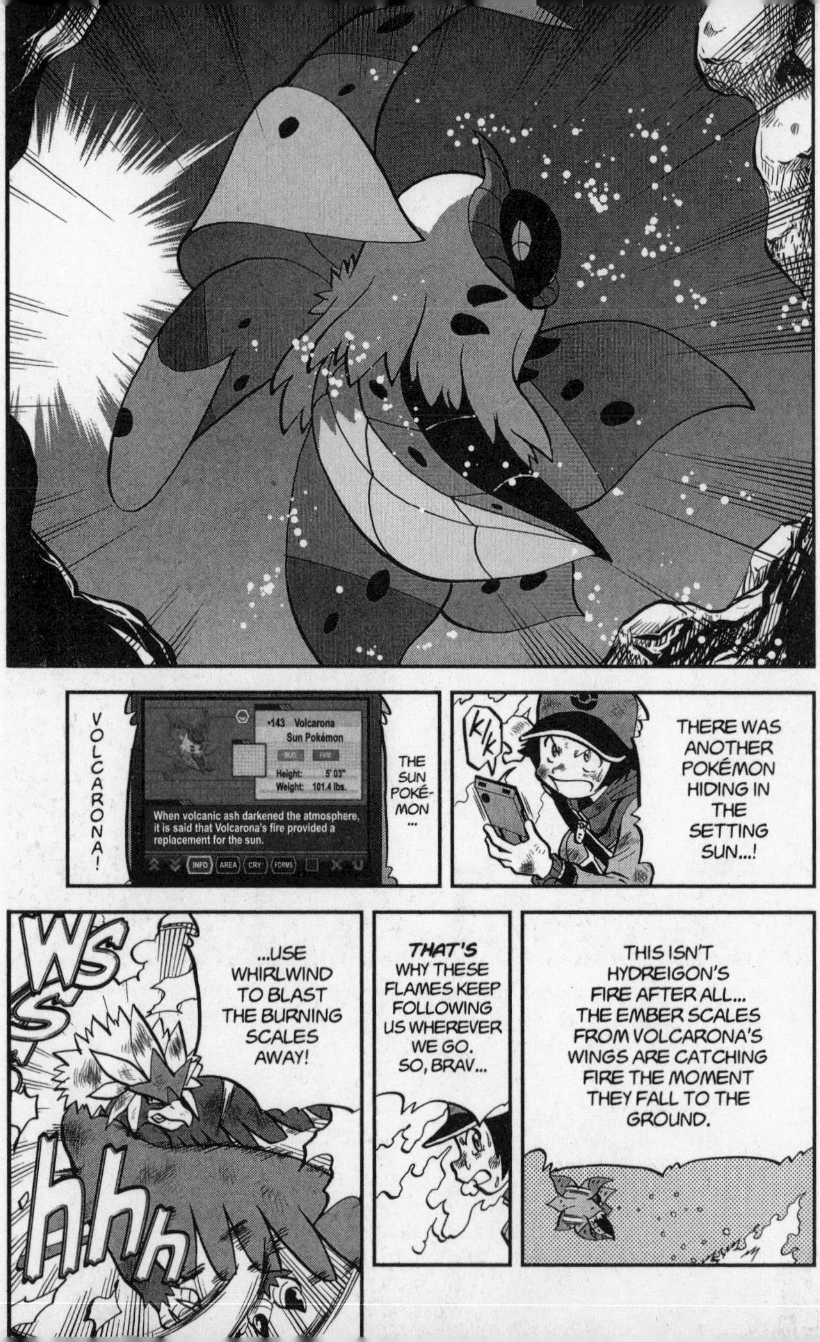
THERE WAS ANOTHER POKÉMON HIDING IN THE SETTING SUN...!
THE SUN POKÉMON...
VOLCARONA!
•143 Volcarona
Sun Pokémon
BUG
FIRE
Height: 5' 03"
Weight: 101.4 lbs.
When volcanic ash darkened the atmosphere, it is said that Volcarona's fire provided a replacement for the sun.
INFO
AREA
CRY
FORMS
THIS ISN'T HYDREIGON'S FIRE AFTER ALL... THE EMBER SCALES FROM VOLCARONA'S WINGS ARE CATCHING FIRE THE MOMENT THEY FALL TO THE GROUND.
THAT'S WHY THESE FLAMES KEEP FOLLOWING US WHEREVER WE GO. SO, BRAV...
...USE WHIRLWIND TO BLAST THE BURNING SCALES AWAY!
WSS
hhh

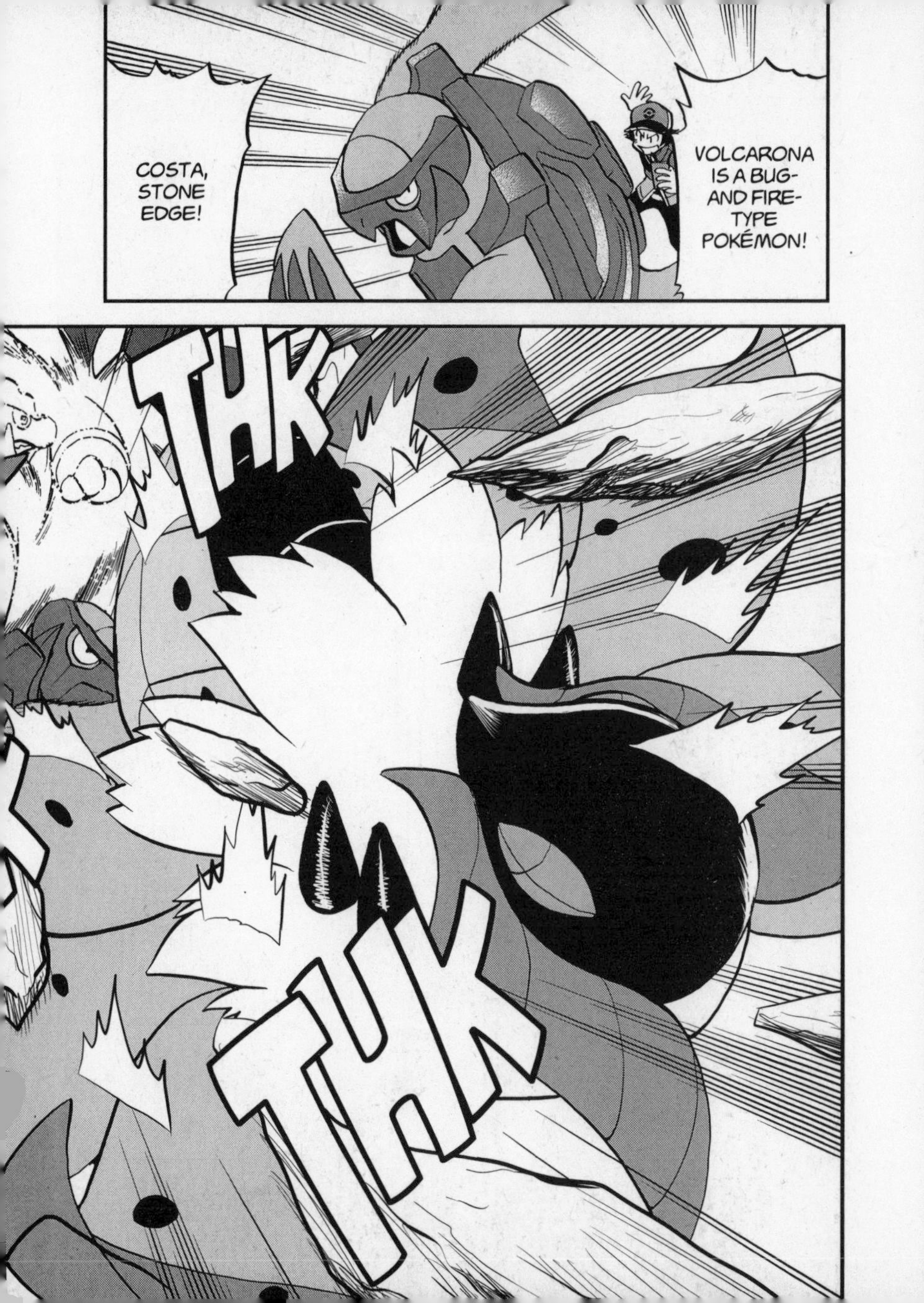
VOLCARONA IS A BUG- AND FIRE- TYPE POKÉMON!
COSTA, STONE EDGE!
THK
THK

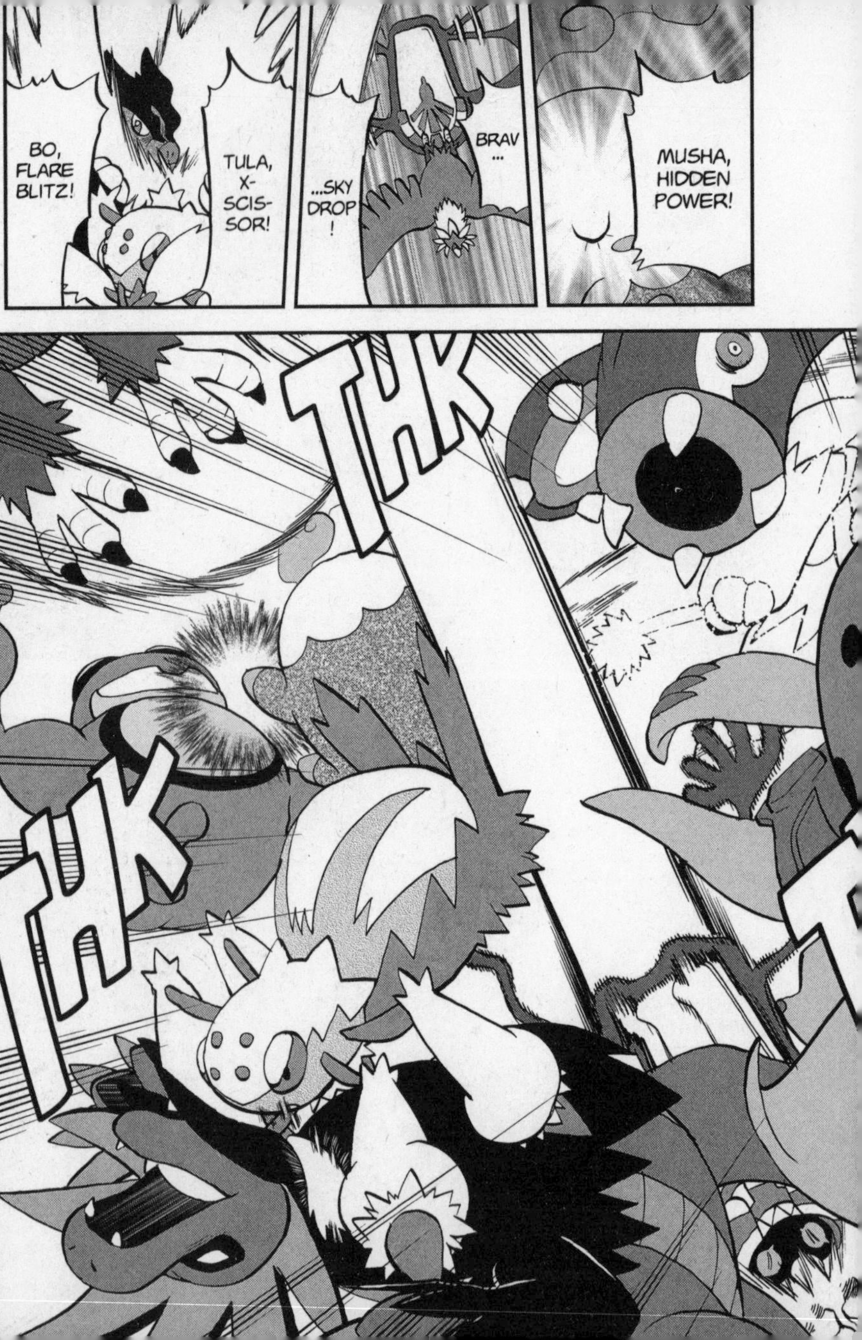
MUSHA, HIDDEN POWER!
BRAV ...
...SKY DROP !
TULA, X-SCISSOR!
BO, FLARE BLITZ!
THK
THK

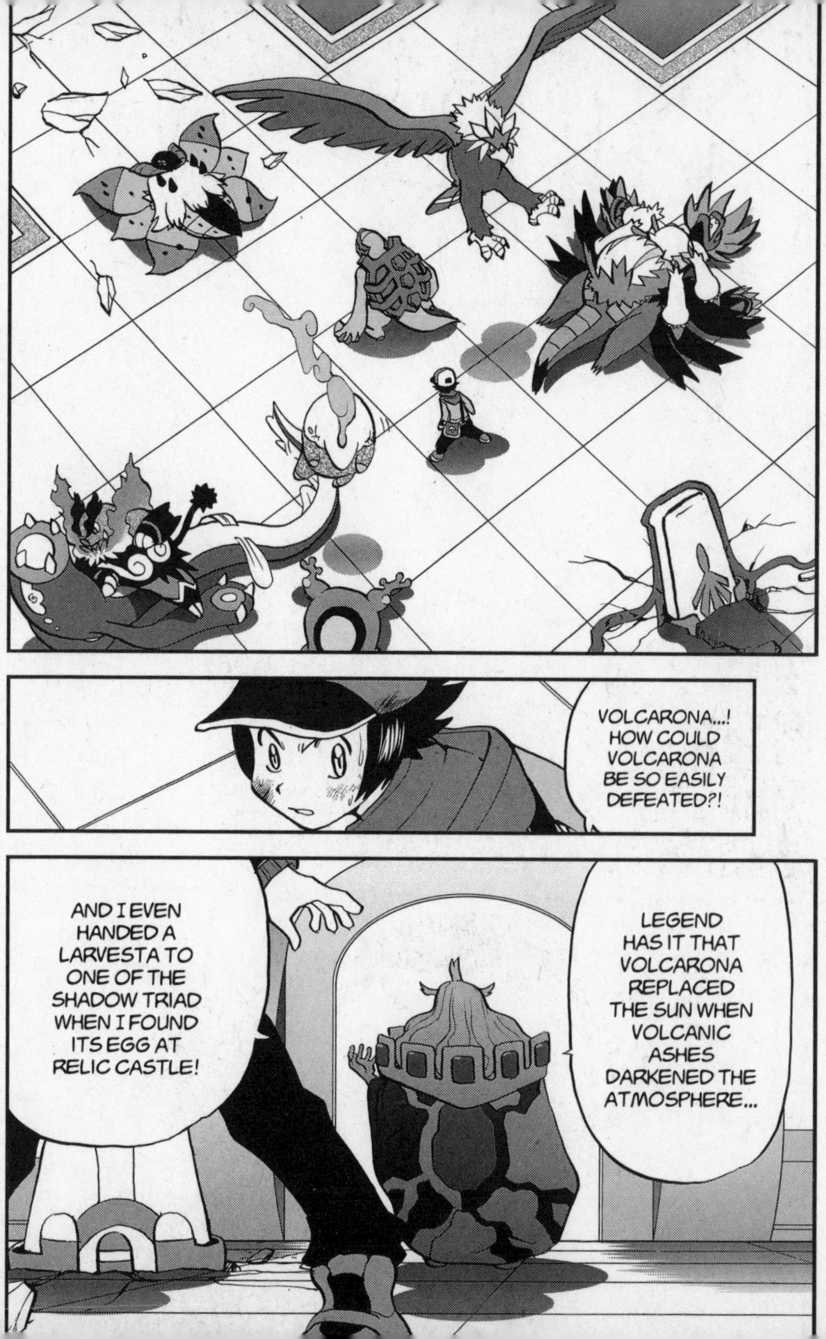
VOLCARONA...! HOW COULD VOLCARONA BE SO EASILY DEFEATED?!
LEGEND HAS IT THAT VOLCARONA REPLACED THE SUN WHEN VOLCANIC ASHES DARKENED THE ATMOSPHERE...
AND I EVEN HANDED A LARVESTA TO ONE OF THE SHADOW TRIAD WHEN I FOUND ITS EGG AT RELIC CASTLE!

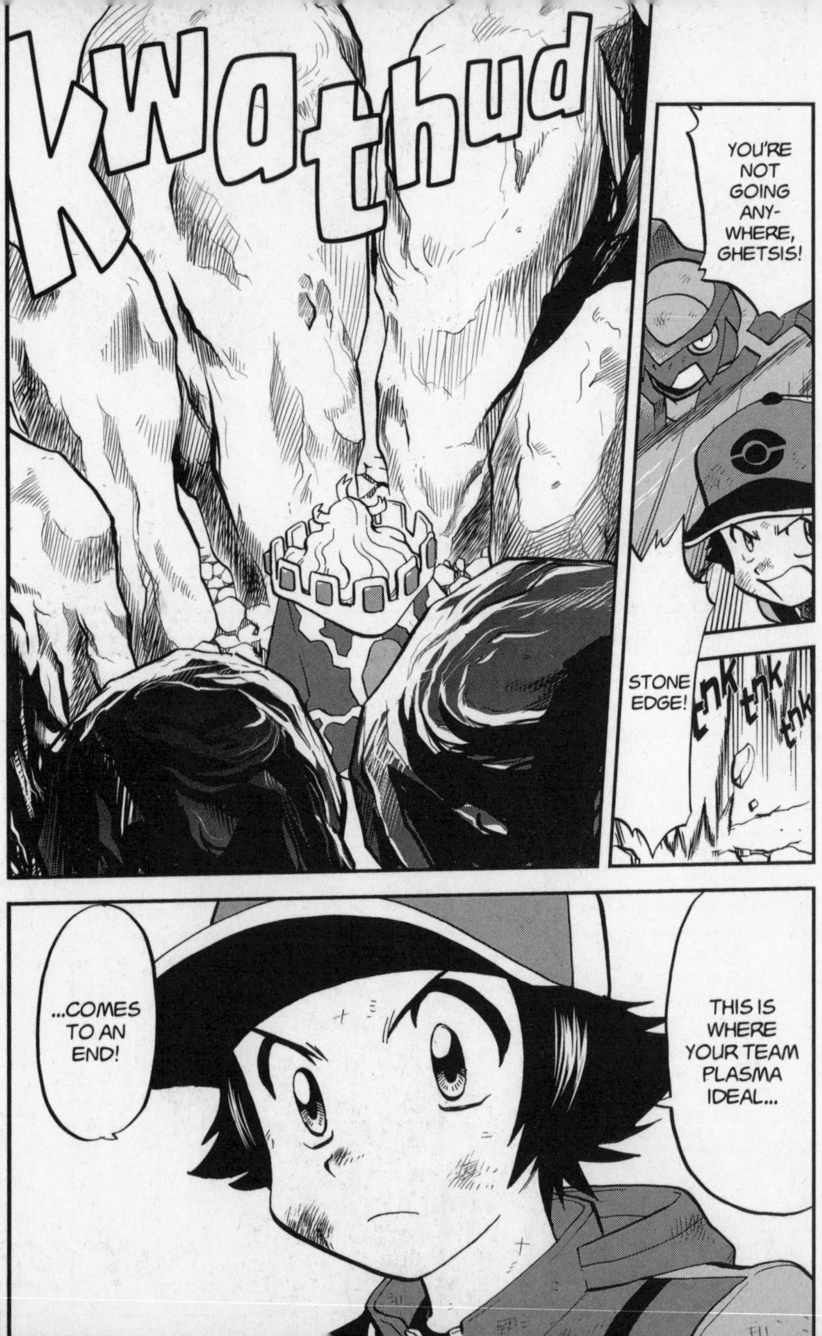
YOU'RE NOT GOING ANY-WHERE, GHETSIS!
STONE EDGE!
tnk tnk tnk
KWATHUD
THIS IS WHERE YOUR TEAM PLASMA IDEAL...
...COMES TO AN END!

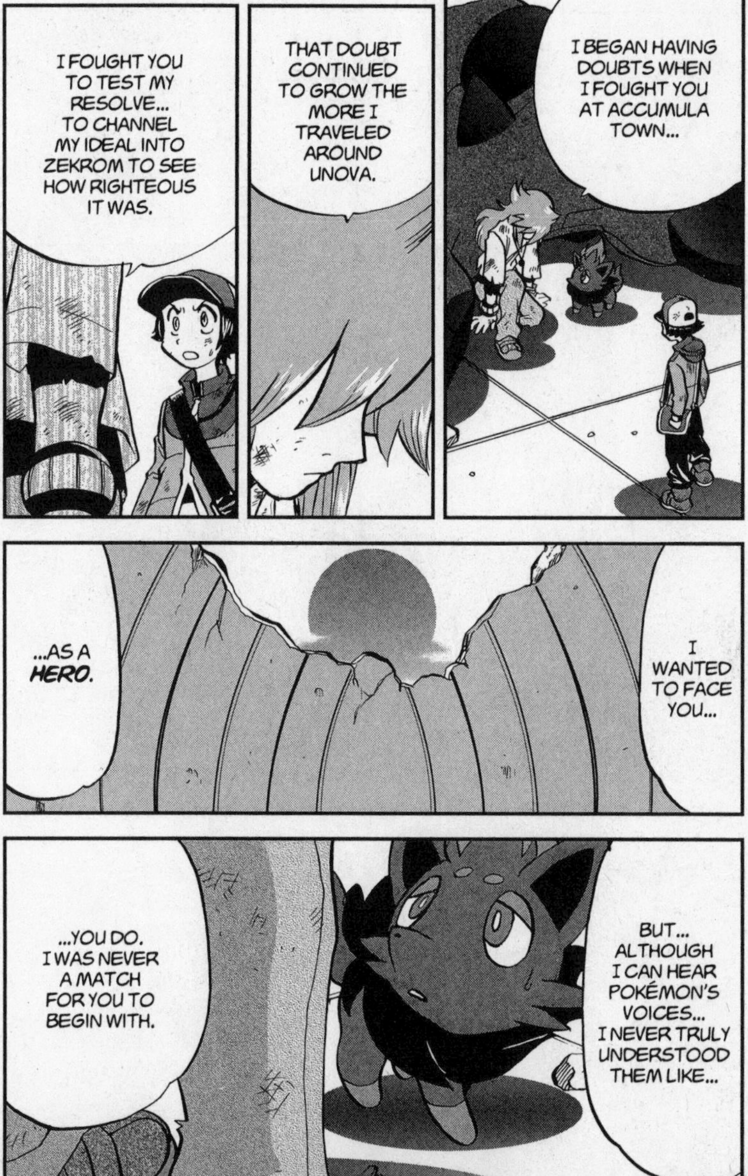
I BEGAN HAVING DOUBTS WHEN I FOUGHT YOU AT ACCUMULA TOWN...
THAT DOUBT CONTINUED TO GROW THE MORE I TRAVELED AROUND UNOVA.
I FOUGHT YOU TO TEST MY RESOLVE... TO CHANNEL MY IDEAL INTO ZEKROM TO SEE HOW RIGHTEOUS IT WAS.
I WANTED TO FACE YOU...
...AS A ***HERO***.
BUT... ALTHOUGH I CAN HEAR POKÉMON'S VOICES... I NEVER TRULY UNDERSTOOD THEM LIKE...
...YOU DO. I WAS NEVER A MATCH FOR YOU TO BEGIN WITH.

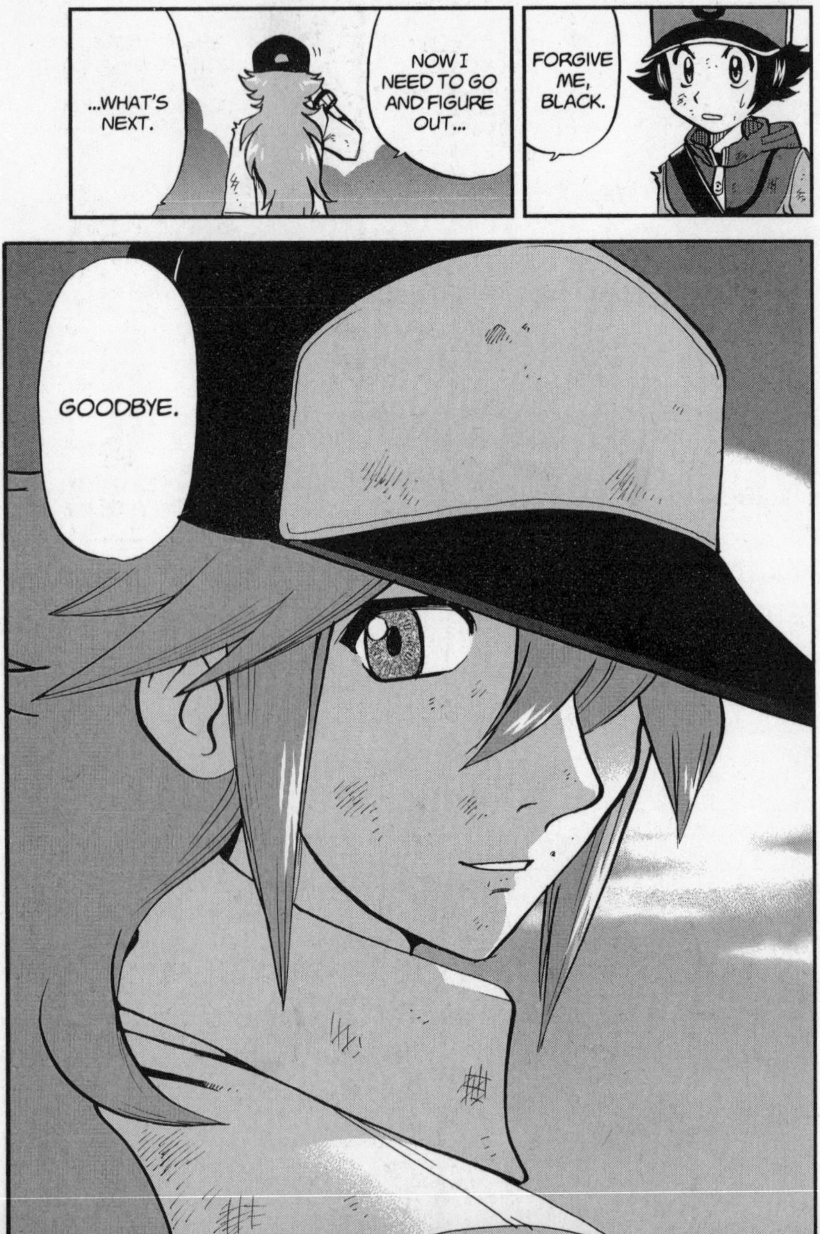
FORGIVE ME, BLACK.
NOW I NEED TO GO AND FIGURE OUT...
...WHAT'S NEXT.
GOODBYE.

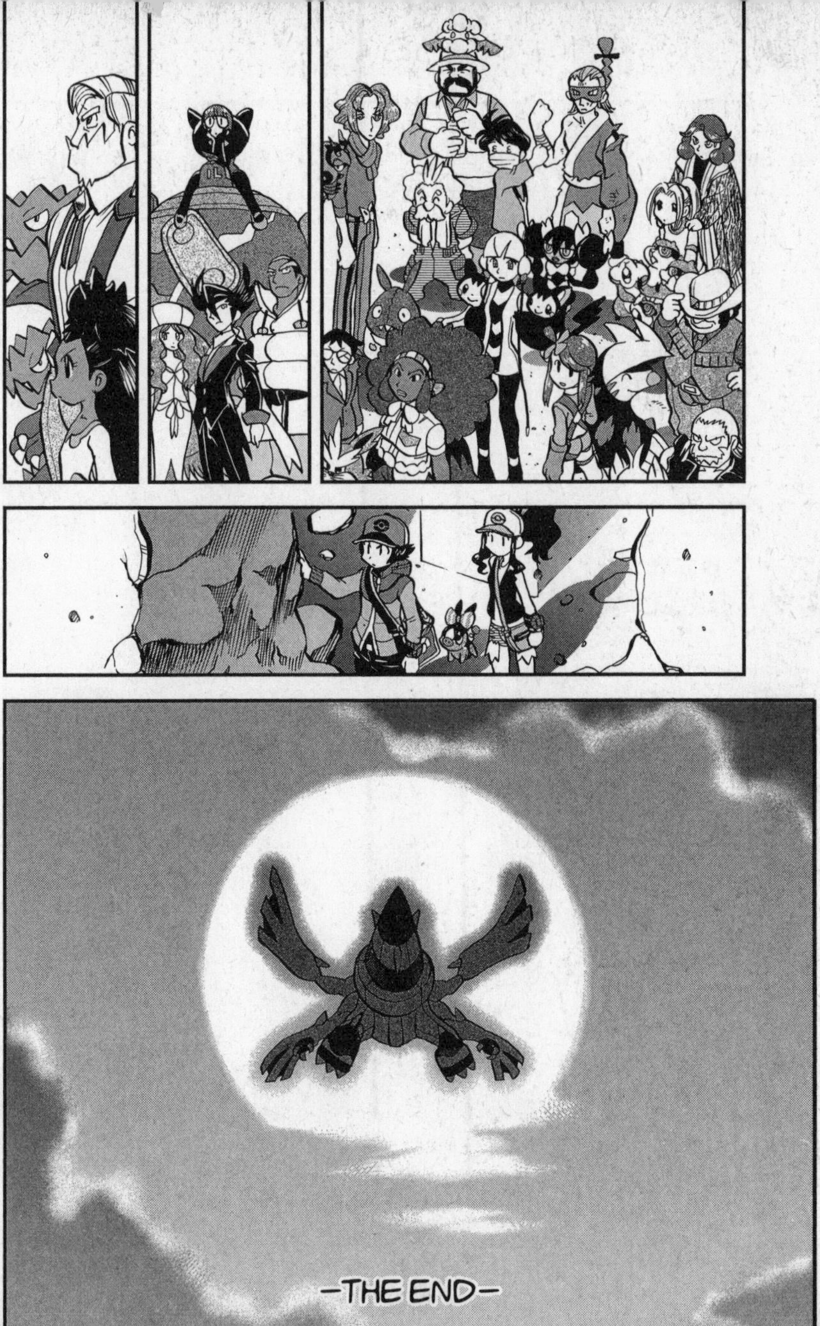
-THE END-

The adventure continues in the Johto region!

POKÉMON™

ADVENTURES™

GOLD & SILVER BOX SET

Includes **POKÉMON ADVENTURES** Vols. 8-14 and a collectible poster!

Story by
HIDENORI KUSAKA

Art by
MATO, SATOSHI YAMAMOTO

More exciting Pokémon adventures starring Gold and his rival Silver! First someone steals Gold's backpack full of Poké Balls (and Pokémon!). Then someone steals Prof. Elm's Totodile. Can Gold catch the thief—or thieves?!

Keep an eye on Team Rocket, Gold... Could they be behind this crime wave?

PERFECT SQUARE

www.viz.com

What's Better Than Catching Pokémon?

Becoming one!

POKéMON
Mystery Dungeon
GINJI'S RESCUE TEAM

Ginji is a normal boy until the day he turns into a Torchic and joins Mudkip's Rescue Team. Now he must help any and all Pokémon in need...but will Ginji be able to rescue his human self?

Become part of the adventure—and mystery—with *Pokémon Mystery Dungeon: Ginji's Rescue Team.* Buy yours today!

www.pokemon.com

POKéMON
Mystery Dungeon
GINJI'S RESCUE TEAM

Inspired by
the brand-new
Nintendo games!
RED RESCUE TEAM
BLUE RESCUE TEAM

Story and art by
Makoto Mizobuchi

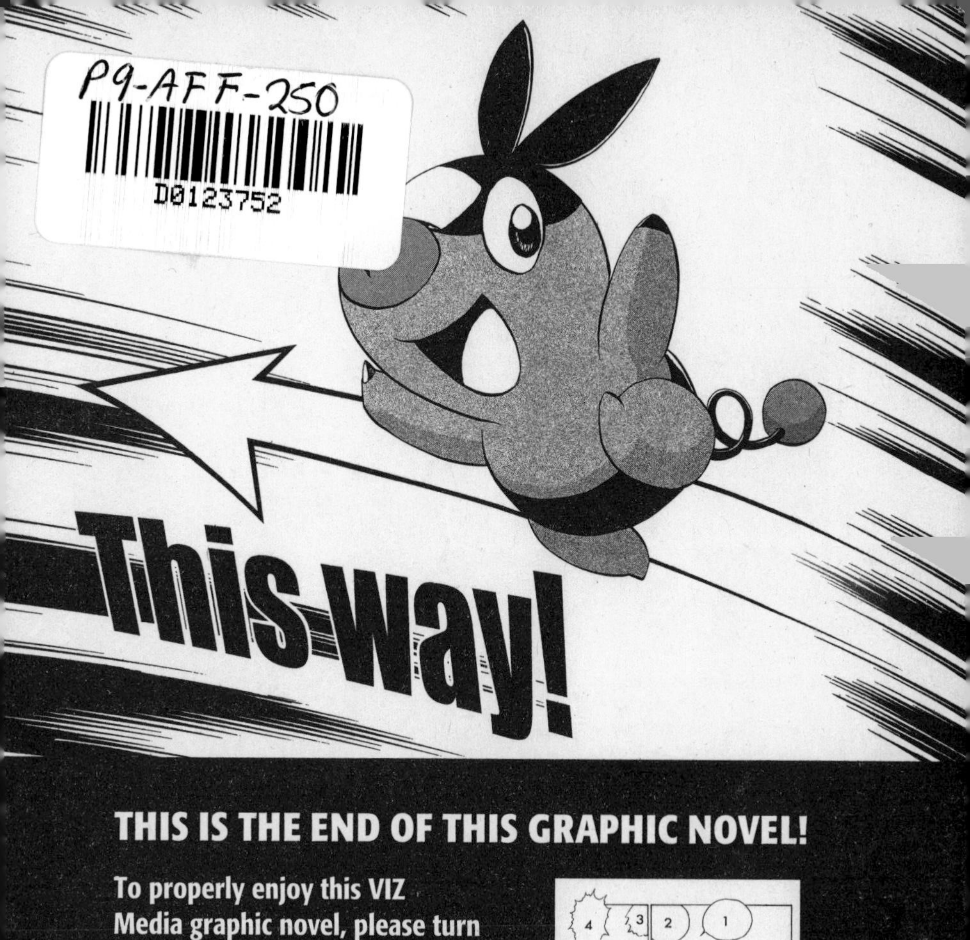
This way!

THIS IS THE END OF THIS GRAPHIC NOVEL!

To properly enjoy this VIZ Media graphic novel, please turn it around and begin reading from right to left.

This book has been printed in the original Japanese format in order to preserve the orientation of the original artwork. Have fun with it!

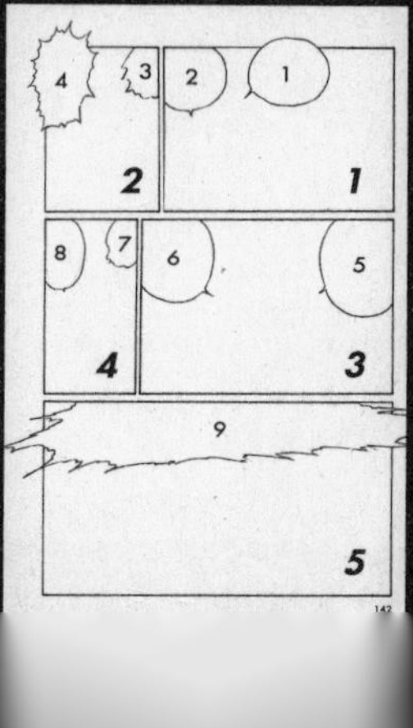
1
2
3
4
1
2
5
6
7
8
3
4
9
5